HIGH
PEAKS

THE
RED
CLIFFS
✚
THE
VILLAGE ✚

VALLEY

THE FIRE MOUNTAINS

THE SALT LAKE

TO THE SECOND AND
THIRD VALLEYS

FRANCE
THE ALPS

ATLANTIC OCEAN

THE PYRENEES

PORTUGAL

SPAIN

ITALY

CORSICA

BALEARIC IS.

GIBRALTAR

SARDINIA

MEDITERRANEAN SEA

SICILY

ATLAS MTS.

AFRICA

*This is the familiar map of the same area today.*

Greetings to Slim and Alix
from
Frank Barringer.

# AND THE WATERS PREVAILED

# and the Prevailed

## D. MOREAU BARRINGER

Illustrated by P. A. Hutchison

E. P. Dutton & Co., Inc., New York

To the late
OWEN WISTER
and his daughter
MARINA
IN APPRECIATION OF THEIR ENCOURAGEMENT

Pre-eminent among the friends who have helped me with this book, I would like to acknowledge my debt to Professor Walter Phelps Hall of Princeton, not only for his invaluable aid but for a long and valued friendship.

# AND THE WATERS PREVAILED

*Over the wide plain around them drifted a lonely wolf-cry.*

THE TIME for the manhood hunt had come, and the boys who were to take part in it sat in the darkness of one end of the bachelors' house. With the rising of the sun they were to take the first steps of their lives as men. Unarmed, naked, alone, they were to go forth from the village to prove their strength and skill against a world from which henceforth they must gain their living. A Spartan test it might have been called, save for the fact that Sparta lay unconceived beyond twelve thousand years of misty future. Five hundred generations of men must rise and fight and learn and die, before their accumulated knowledge and strength could bring forth those ancient glories that seem now to be at the merest threshold of the race's past. Thebes, Ur of the Chaldees, Troy—the peoples that were to write these names boldly upon history had not yet learned to build for themselves the lowliest shelter of mud or thatch.

Andor the Little, trying to be inconspicuous but at the same time one of the group, hugged his thin knees and braced his back against the wall. Eager as he was to join the excited talk of the morrow, he could not help wincing at the thought of the ceaseless teasing that his small size and slight figure brought down on him. Stor the Strong, the biggest of the boys, was also Andor's chief tormentor; and painful experience had shown Andor that it was impossible for him to beat Stor in a fight. It was better, he had learned, to draw as little attention to himself as possible.

And so Andor said nothing, but listened avidly. Out of the darkness Stor spoke.

"I shall bring home the skin of a dog wolf," he said, "and a long spear like Arran's. Nobody else except Arran and me could wield so heavy a spear. I shall be as great a hunter as the Manslayer himself."

"Be sure that there isn't a wolf puppy around when you kill the dog wolf," said Kelan, "or you might get bitten and have to run the way you did the last time."

There was a burst of embarrassed laughter. The incident had become well known, although no one but Kelan the Merry, with his happy touch of banter that failed to offend, would have dared refer to it. Stor glowered and made a threatening gesture, but the spell of the evening lay heavy on the boys, and the usual explosive fight did not ensue. Kelan spoke again, his eyes on the blue-black distance beyond the doorway.

"I would rather be like Mertan the Swift," he said. "Mertan

could outrun a yearling colt and bring its carcass home as quickly as he had chased it. He could jump like the red deer, so far and so fast that he could catch a duck before it left the water. Arran could kill a wolf or a man, but Mertan brought home the best meat."

Eltan's uncertain voice came from a corner, where he had curled his plump body on the floor. "I want to be like Calin the Crafty," he said, "and build snares and traps for the animals. I once built a pool for trout, and would have caught many big ones if Stor hadn't frightened them all away. I shall do that again, when he can't see me, and I'll set sharp sticks to catch rabbits, as Calin did. Then I shall eat meat when all of you are starving on berries, waiting for dog wolves or red deer."

"Andor keeps his mouth shut," said Stor. "Why don't you speak, Andor, and say what you will be like when you come home a man?"

"I don't know," said Andor, glad for the darkness, as he felt his face grow hot. Lost in reverie he mused on the village where he lived, the river below it sweeping silently through its willows, and the peaks of the ice-crowned mountains far to the Northwest. He thought of those frozen forest fastnesses whence came the tribe's ancestors to settle in the valley near the broad river whose waters teemed with fish. How he would like to explore those mountains. Perhaps some day he would if only he acquitted himself well in the hunt.

Stor, with clumsy sarcasm, returned to the baiting. "I suppose tomorrow, Andor," he said, "you will fight off a whole pack of wolves and clothe yourself and all your wives in their fur."

"Oh let him alone," said Kelan the Merry. "If he can't hunt tomorrow he'll die and you'll be rid of him. If he can, and comes home with a fox or a wolf he may become a great hunter after all."

"Great hunter," snarled Stor. "It takes a man to be a great hunter. He won't even be able to kill a rabbit."

Andor remained silent. Tonight the edge of Stor's tongue could not cut through the glory of the great evening. The voices, childishly boastful or shaky with excitement, went on, but Andor's dreams armored him against them.

Outside the night had grown to full stature, and the little group of mud houses lay silent under the stars. Over the wide plain around them drifted a lonely wolf-cry—assured and proud of its domination. To the wolves there was no terror in the little tribe of men—they only saw another animal that disputed their mastery over the game herds. Except for the pieces of stone which men carried so unaccountably, their armament was feeble—short teeth, no claws at all, and only two legs with which to run. How could the wolves see inside those curious bulging heads that men had, and guess that therein lay a weapon mightier than any claw or fang—a weapon that in the end would conquer, not only wolves, but all the world as well?

As though the wolf-call were a signal, the older men broke up the talk, called to the boys to go to bed. "You will need your strength in the morning, youngsters," said old Iri, his deep tones in contrast to the boys' excited tenors.

Stor growled, "When I come home he won't speak to me like that," but obediently he lay down beside the others. The flashing stars moved slowly overhead, lighting the sleeping horses

**12**

and bison and antelope on the grassy plains. They revealed as well the movement of certain unsleeping ones—wolves that prowled singly or in packs, lions from the south, whose voices shattered the horses' sleep. Northward, in the forests and ranges that still were choked with snow, the starlight glittered on the fantastic tusks of a woolly, bear-shaped mammoth, and revealed the gray backs of a herd of reindeer, motionless in the cold.

With so much game, large and small, and with roots and berries to pick, a boy could only fail on his manhood hunt because of such a lack of skill or strength or courage that the tribe could well dispense with him.

The coming of day was heralded by a cooling of the air, as the dawn wind moved out of the west. Long before light, the boys gathered by the walls of the bachelor's house, while Talgar the Wise, chief of the tribe by virtue of strength and wisdom, built with his own hands the sacred fire. By twos and threes the men gathered, the women and children forming silent outer circles. Firelight glowed on smooth shoulders and long, straight legs, and left darker by contrast the men's curly beards and wide, matted chests. Nearly three hundred people were ringed about the growing fire. In the background the women's strong-boned faces were dimly seen, but their lithe bodies, clad only in skirts of deerskin, were shadowed by the men grouped closer to the flame.

**13**

Talgar arranged before the fire the sacred symbols of the tribe. The wing of an owl, the hoof of an antelope, and the jaw of a wolf came first. Then followed a shining spearhead of obsidian, a dark clod of dried mud, and a short pointed stick. Last was a rounded black boulder, which he drew from a sack of wolf-skin and placed reverently on the ground before him.

Talgar sat down, facing the boys, who stood with their backs to the bachelors' house. Behind Talgar sat the Old Men, whose office it was to chant the ritual songs, to learn and to recite the legends of the old time. The firelight was gentle to their chiseled faces, and disguised the gray streaks on crown and jaw and chest.

Softly, in the stillness that awaited morning, they began their chant. As they sang they beat the slow tempo on the ground with the knuckles of their closed fists.

"The moon of the melting
Has opened and closed.
The moon of the winds
Has opened and closed.
The moon of the leaves
Has opened and closed.
The forest is ready
To shelter the deer.
The young men have grown.
Their arms are needed.
Their feet are stamping.
Their spears are sharp.
They watch in the sky
For the moon of the ripening
To open and close.

Go into the forest
Lake Arran the Slayer.
Live in the forest
Like Elor the Rover.
Come from the forest
Like Mertan the Swift.
Then the moon of the pairing
Will open and close,
And the moon of the building
Will open and close,
And the moon of love
Will open . . . and . . . close."

The chant, never rising above a subdued hum, died to a whisper. The boys stole glances at each other and shifted their feet. Talgar arose and mended the fire, so that the renewed flames threw the boys' shadows in shivering outlines on the walls. The chant began again.

"The young women call
The men that are coming.
The old women mourn
The boys that are going.
The skin of the kill
And the weapons of stone
Herald the changes
That mark them as men.
The Old Man looks down
From the Darkness-by-day
And beats on the tusk
That troubles the sky,
Seeing the young men
Safe in the forest,

Seeing the young men
Killing the deer.
He casts down shreds
Of the sun that he hides
And beats on the tusk
That troubles the sky
Glad that the young men
Conquer the forest."

The drone of the chant drugged the boys' senses and stimulated their dreams. Andor, swaying unconsciously to the thudding rhythm, thought of the Old Man who dwelt in thunderstorms.

A subtle change came over the sky, and the stars seemed to slip deeper into its paling blue. A breath of wind stole over the rapt circle, and the fire flutteringly bowed to it.

Then Talgar arose, and motioned the boys to come closer to him. "Boys," he said, "for you are still boys this morning, today you go out to show us that you are men. Heretofore you have been children, eating the meat of other men's kills. If, indeed, you have sometimes caught your own food, you have done so from sport and not necessity. Henceforth it will be in earnest.

"Today you will go out from the village," continued Talgar, "and you will not return until you can bring with you proof of your power in the hunt. You must not return until the moon-door opens once in the sky and closes again as it is closed tonight. Then, if you have eaten well, and have clothed yourselves in the warm skin of a beast you have slain, you may return, to take your places as men in the village, and choose a wife from among the old men's daughters.

*16*

"And you must hunt alone," went on the quiet, heavy voice. "You may meet one another, and speak, and even camp together. But you must ask or give no assistance in the chase or the kill, in the fashioning of weapons or the curing of a skin. None of you may accept food from another, or a weapon, or so much as a stone.

"If the skill, the speed, or the strength of any of you is not sufficient to conquer the animals of the plains, and when another moon closes you know that you cannot live in the forest, you may come back to the village. But you will ever afterward be treated as Kaka the Witless. You will clean the houses and the hearths, and men will smile at you as you do so. None of the women will go near you, so that you will never have children to disgrace the tribe as you have done. If such a one is found with a woman, he will be killed."

Silent were the unmoving boys; silent the massed ranks of men with spears and women with children in their arms. Not a baby whimpered, for they had been trained from their earliest infancy not to cry. The flame of the ceremonial fire struggled in the cool wind and paled before the growing light. Andor's spine tingled at the old man's words. He knew he could not fail. He imagined great deeds of prowess. In the uncertain light he met the eyes of his widowed mother, beseeching and heartening at the same time. He felt the presence of his father, that father who had died five years before. He forgot that he was called Andor the Little, that the boys of his own age delighted in his persecution. He only knew that he was beginning his life, and that it would be glorious.

Now Talgar stooped to the objects ranged before the fire. As

*Firelight glowed on smooth shoulders and long, straight legs.*

19

he picked up the wolf-jaw the boys all extended their right arms. Talgar walked slowly before them, and struck each extended arm lightly with the jaw, so that the teeth left a little row of red marks.

"Gray wolf," he said, "those who have felt your teeth in death will not fear them in life. Send your strength into these boys, that as men they shall be stronger than you."

Talgar laid down the jaw, covering it as he did so with a deerskin. Then he took the antelope hoof, and brushed with it the toes of the boys' extended feet. "Their feet have caught you in death, tall antelope," said he. "Lead them now in life, that as men they shall be swifter than you."

Followed the owl's wing. "They have heard the rush of your dead feathers, dark owl. Make their ears keen to hear them in life, that as men the least sound of the forest shall be clearer to them than to you. Make their step more silent than your soundless wing."

He picked up the pointed fire-stick, such a stick as they had all used to spin in a hole in a dry log to start a fire. The boys passed it silently from hand to hand.

"Falun, bringer of fire," cried the old man, "let your wisdom follow these boys, that as men they will never want for warmth."

He returned the blackened stick to the row, covering it with the deerskin. Next the spearhead was handed down the line. "Magri, shaper of stones, teach these boys your craft, that as men they shall never want for a weapon. Make them strong of body and arm, as you were."

The clod of earth went around. It was dried hard by the sun, and rounded by the touch of many hands. "Hastor, builder of houses," chanted the chief, "bestow your vision upon these boys, that as men they shall not want for shelter. Make them wise to rule their tribe, and keep the peace, as you were."

Last he picked up the rounded black boulder. With both hands he raised and held it over his head. The full light of day was in the sky, and as he spoke the first sunlight warmed the black mass of rock in his hands.

"Old Man," he cried, "Old Man with one eye, who watches the caves of the old time, here are more boys grown to man-hood. Watch them as you watched their fathers. Send them your spotted deer and your tall antelope for food. Hide them from the lion's claw and from the keen-eyed wolf pack. Let the rain of your clouds bring grass on the hills so that game may be plentiful and fat. Feed them by your rushing rivers. Clothe them against your mountain breath. Give them the stuff of life, and if they are men they will make life of it."

With a grunt he dropped the rock at his feet, and then straightened and looked sharply at the boys. "Now go," he said.

The renewed chant of the gray men was drowned in the women's excited whispering or sobbing. Turning their backs on the climbing sun the boys filed from the circle. Self-consciously, holding their heads high, their bodies ruddy with morning, they passed from view behind the long house.

Each following his own long-meditated plan, some headed for the level plains to the east; others, including Andor, swam the cold river and emerged, silvered with spray, on the farther shore. There they separated. The villagers watched them as one by one they faded into the forest patches, or disappeared from view into some fold of the plain.

For hours Andor walked, his shadow growing shorter before him. At length he stopped, and saw that he had come into a sunny glade, surrounded by a thinly-sown forest of juniper and pine. In the glade were thickets of blackberries. Andor ate hungrily, and cooled his feet in a little trickle of stream.

Then he followed his plan. He broke a young sapling, a green stick whose end split as he twisted off the leafy part. He chose a wedge-shaped stone, and stuck it into the split part of the stick, tying it with strips of bark. It made a hammer-like weapon, its slender shaft about three feet long, with a springiness pleasant to the hand. The bark wrappings were rather insecure, but he thought it would serve until he found something better.

He had thought of using this throwing-hammer to secure a rabbit, but it was far too early to find one, except by merest accident. So, idly swinging his hammer, he started up the bed of a stream, looking for flint for a knife or spearhead. Before long he found what he wanted. It was an oval pebble of gray chert, as long as his extended hand. He managed to break it into three pieces on a bigger rock, and then, concealing himself under a low-branched tree, he began chipping the pieces to make an edge.

It was a long and tedious job, so he let his eyes wander while he worked. After an hour or more of alternate chipping and peering from his retreat, he saw a dark form, far out across the sun-drenched plain.

It was a man, but no such man as Andor knew at home. He was much smaller than the village men, and his skin was black. He walked with a seemingly careless gait, but his head swung constantly to right and left, obviously on the alert. He carried no weapons, and wore no clothes of any kind.

Andor stopped work, and stretched himself flat on the ground, his head concealed by a trailing branch. The black stranger might be a small man, by village standards, but Andor was a fifteen year old boy, and a slight one at that. Obviously he must try to avoid detection.

The strange man came rapidly nearer, until Andor could see his woolly hair and glistening eyes. He was coming straight for Andor's tree. Closer and closer he came, growing more cautious as he neared the grove. At last he stopped, and sniffed the air in all directions, like a fox. Andor's heart jumped violently when he saw the man start, and look steadily at his hiding place.

He must have been discovered, and there was nothing for it but to fight it out. Still Andor remained flattened on the ground, waiting until the last possible moment in the hope that he had not been observed after all.

No thought but fighting entered Andor's head. His tribe never considered that other peoples could be anything but enemies. Other white men were so few and lived so far away, that none had been encountered in recent years. The dwarfish black men, on the other hand, were considered only as dangerous animals. They spoke no intelligible language, they lived entirely in the open, knowing nothing of building or even of caves, and they fashioned no weapons, using only stones picked up at random. Whenever encountered, they either showed fight—as this one seemed to—or fled in terror.

A curious fear gripped Andor's belly. Cautiously he tightened his grip on the hammer and worked his left hand under his chest, to aid him in springing to his feet when the moment came.

The black man, never taking his eyes from Andor's hiding place, squatted on his heels and felt about him for a rock. Now was the moment, before he found a weapon.

With a yell which he tried to make deep and terrifying Andor leaped at him. His hammer whirled once around his head, and flew straight at the gleaming white teeth that flashed before him. He covered the space between them in two strides and was at the black throat before he could see what damage his hammer had done.

The black man rose to his feet in time to meet him, and they locked. Andor's impact was enough to roll his enemy over backward, and he found himself sitting astride the black chest, one hand gripping his enemy's bearded throat, the other groping for his hammer. The black man's feet kicked uselessly, and one hand tore at Andor's wrist. The other, Andor suddenly saw, lay beside him helplessly, blood oozing from a jagged wound on the wrist. The hammer had taken effect, then.

But despite his injury the enemy, a grown man, was Andor's

**24**

superior in strength. Before Andor could find his hammer the man had rolled him over, and groped for his throat with his good hand, his taloned fingers wrapped around Andor's windpipe. Andor knew he could not survive long under that grip. Then he thought of the injured wrist. With his free hand Andor seized and twisted it. The grating of the broken bone was too much for the black man, who screamed in pain and released Andor's throat to defend himself. Again Andor twisted, and the fight went out of his enemy on the instant. He sprang up to get away, but Andor, his joy in the battle returning, brought the man down with an arm around his leg. At the same moment his groping fingers found the hammer shaft. Rising to his knees, Andor struck, with all the swing of his wiry back and arms. The battle was over. Quivering with excitement, Andor looked alternately at the dead man in front of him, and at his useless hammer—its handle split and its bark strings snapped by the force of the blow. Then a voice called his name.

He wheeled, and faced Kelan—a very breathless and rather pale Kelan, whose eyes glistened with excitement.

"I saw it all," he panted. "It was a great fight! Andor, you are a real fighter after all. Wait until I tell this at home."

"But how did you come here?" asked Andor, a little stupidly. The reaction of the battle was gripping him, and his hand and voice were shaky.

"Just as you did," replied Kelan. "Oh, that was a fight. You broke his arm with your hammer, and then you used his broken arm to make him let you go. How did you think of that? Nobody else would have. Andor the Black-slayer. That's what they'll call you."

Flushed with the victory, they sought the brook, leaving the enemy's body to the hyenas, and Andor washed the sand and blood from his bruised face. To the cuts he paid no attention. They would be healed by morning. The crude surgery over, Andor looked ruefully at his ruined hammer.

"Where is your weapon, Kelan?" he asked. "Mine's broken."

"Oh, I haven't any," answered the other. "I can live for a while on berries, and make one later. We have a whole month, you know. There's no hurry."

Andor looked at his friend in admiration of such confidence. That was the right attitude, he felt, and not the worriedly conscientious one that he could not help adopting. Nevertheless, the details of the plan he had formed seemed urgent. He was going to kill a rabbit with his hammer, and use its hide or its gut as lashings for a new and better weapon.

Kelan had other ideas. "Let's eat some berries," he suggested, "and find a place to sleep. We can look for tools tomorrow. Perhaps we might camp together for a few days."

At this Andor hardly dared speak. Kelan the Merry, the carefree associate of the great figures in his boy's world, was suggesting to Andor the Little that they camp together. It was too wonderful to believe. "All right, we might," said Andor, carefully offhand. But his head was high, and the forest, turning darker under the declining sun, was lit by a new and indescribable glow.

Sleep refused to come with the darkness. Andor's excitement held his fatigue in check, and Kelan, tall and wiry, had

had an easy day. Like schoolboys they lay on their backs in the pine needles, while their talk ranged unbridled over the land.

Kelan opened a subject that apparently had worked in his mind before.

"Last night Stor said he wanted to be like Arran the Man-slayer, and fat little Eltan said he wanted to be like Calin the Crafty, and I said I wanted to be like Mertan the Swift. When they asked what you thought, you said you didn't know. Why did you say that?"

Andor felt a sudden rush of desire to unburden himself to this new-won friend. He had always admired and envied Kelan, with his easy skill at everything he undertook, and his laughing friendliness to everyone. But never before had he thought of telling him—or of telling anyone except his mother —the strange feelings he had when he listened to the old-time songs.

"This morning Talgar spoke of Hastor, the builder of houses," he said. "Have you heard the old men sing of Hastor?"

"No," answered Kelan. "Hastor always made me tired. When they sang about him I went out to catch trout in the river. What did he do? While the other men were hunting he sat and played with the mud. He built houses, but what do we need with houses, when the broad pine branches make a better roof? Who cares whether it rains at night? We can always get dry again."

Andor was quick to answer. "Hastor did more than build houses. He made the laws of the tribe. He saw that the boys and single men should live together, and the girls and single women, and that both should live apart from the families and

**27**

*Andor felt a sudden rush of desire to unburden himself to this new-won friend.*

28

their babies. Before he came all the tribe lived together. Girls interfered with the boys' play, babies slept on the hunters' weapons, and they said that men could not trust their wives, living among other men. Quarrels arose, and many men were killed for no good.

"So Hastor divided the people, and built houses to show the division. He brought peace and good hunting to the tribe, where there was only jealousy and fighting before. That is what the old men say.

"I know I cannot be just like Hastor, or do just what he did. He built the village, and it does not need to be done again. He made the laws, and we do not need others. But I want to do something that will make people see that I am not just Andor the Little."

Kelan laughed softly, but not derisively. He sensed the hero worship in Andor's attitude, and it pleased him. But he also had an uneasy sense that there were depths to these thoughts that he had never explored, and that troubled him vaguely. Therefore he laughed. By long experience he knew that his laugh always seemed pleasant to others. It did not bring resentment, as Stor's did, nor indulgent smiles like little Eltan's. It caused other people to laugh, too—not uncomfortably, but happily, because it came from his own happy heart. Andor warmed to the laugh. With breathless thankfulness, he felt that he had found a real friendship.

"Do you see what I mean?" he continued. "I would like to find a great enemy tribe coming to attack the village and know how to turn them away. Or I would like to be the first to see the wolves come down, so that then I could show the hunters where to go to follow the game, and there would be no famine. I think that would be greater than being as strong as Arran or as swift as Mertan."

"Perhaps it would," said Kelan, to whom the thought was new. He had always visioned a hero as a strong, lithe fighter, who brought down a beast of the chase with skill and dispatch, or met his enemy in open fight and killed him with a blow. The picture that the old songs drew of Hastor, squatting by his rows of experimental bricks, so rapt in contemplation that others had to bring him his meat, had seemed silly to him. Perhaps there was a deeper significance in that picture that he had not seen, but that the old men, and Andor, saw. He would try to think it all out, in the morning.

Despite their uneven bed, and their complete nakedness in the cool night breezes, the boys were quickly asleep. It was not the drugged sleep of exhaustion, for no one who slept that way could long survive the dangers of the forest. Instead, each unusual whisper or rustle brought them awake, and dropped them immediately to sleep when it proved to herald no danger. Though their sleep was broken, they rose so refreshed from it that the fatigue of the evening might never have been.

Before the day had paled on the plains, or stolen into the forest fringes, they were up, and had separated for the day's hunting. Andor returned to the scene of his battle, partly to retrieve the flints he had dropped, and partly on the chance of encountering a rabbit. Kelan sought the brook. He chose a rock that jutted over a clear shaded pool, and lay face downward on it, watching for fish. His right hand, holding a stone, was drawn back in readiness to throw.

He waited, tense and silent, while the woods awoke to the movements of the day. The gurgle of the little stream went on unchanged, but other sounds grew over and concealed it, layer by layer. The full spring foliage was swept by the fingers of soft breezes. Sparrows and fly-catchers began their conversations in the branches. A troop of jays, like traveling jesters, swooped through the leaves, infecting the forest with their unbalanced laughter. When they had gone, the somnolent voice of a wood pigeon could be heard.

The stream's banks moved with tiny life. Ants scurried on their engrossing errands, and butterflies idled through the sunrays. A shrew, tiniest of mammals, peered from his dead-leaf house, and sallied forth on some momentous adventure. Kelan could see his trembling whiskers, as he tasted in the air the unfamiliar scent of man. Then a brightly-hued mayfly, miscalculating its erratic flight, struck the surface of the pool with a minute splash. Kelan watched it closely. A shadow sped from the depths of the pool toward it. The trout's splash at the surface was smothered by the greater splash of Kelan's rock. The shrew vanished like magic, the sparrows paused in their chatter, and Kelan's eyes, intent on the disturbed water, crinkled as they spied a silvery streak glimmering in the mud clouds. He retrieved the little trout, and stood up to stretch.

Meanwhile, Andor sat under his pine roof at the edge of the sweeping plain. Here were none of the intimate forest sounds,

**32**

but only a breathless silence, wide as the plain and intangible as the night-shadows deserting the sky. By imperceptible stages the distances became visible, and the colors of the east swam from blue to gray to rose. In the western sky a faint but majestic arc of blue, rimmed with a breath of ashes-of-roses, sank lower as the light increased. It was the earth's own shadow, made visible on the impalpable upper air. As it approached and merged into the hills, a spot on the opposite horizon grew golden, then fiery, and the sun appeared. From far down the slope a pinpoint of sound reached his ear—a click as of stone on stone. Andor's keen eyes, instantly tracing its origin, saw a file of antelope wind from a wrinkle of the plain, heads erect, ears and noses scouting the path. Their delicate horns and slender legs were etched sharply on the gray-green background. They were too far away for pursuit, and Andor's weapon, idle in his grasp, was still too rudimentary to serve. He took up again his rhythmic chipping of the flint.

A rabbit appeared, and Andor changed to a statue in an instant, only his eyes following the rabbit's aimless path. Whenever the rabbit's head was turned away, his right arm swung slowly back to a throwing position; when the rabbit's eyes became visible he stopped again in rigid immobility. His breathing hardly moved the smooth outline of his chest and belly.

At length he judged that the rabbit would come no closer. It was a long throw, but the risk must be taken. His arm whipped past his shoulder, and the flint flashed momentarily in the sun. Then it struck the ground in a clatter of small stones and dust. From the dust cloud the rabbit emerged, ears flat, feet flying faster than the eye could follow. He had missed. He retrieved the flint, and continued his work.

The loss of the rabbit reminded him of his hunger, and he tried to satisfy it at the berry bushes. It was thin fare, and his desire for meat made him abandon work on the flint, and fashion another throwing-hammer like the one that had served him so well the day before.

With this he killed two squirrels. He could not save the skins, for his knife was not finished, but the raw meat and blood were stimulating. He extracted the intestines and found that they made tough and serviceable cord. With it he replaced the grass and bark on his light hammer, and was much more satisfied. The day passed with more work on the flint, and another unsuccessful attempt at a rabbit.

When the sun swung down to the mountains that day, a silver sliver of moon followed it to rest. The fact that that sliver must grow to a full circle, and dwindle again to nothingness before their trial was over, oppressed the boys not at all. They sat under the darkling branches, and in low voices recounted the day, and spun glorious futures, as at millions of sunsets millions of boys have done, before and since.

"North and west," said Kelan, "there is always forest. It leads up to the mountains, to the very feet of the Ice Mountains where the Old Man sits. I think it is the best way to go. There are many streams, and trout in every one. That is the easiest hunting."

"But you can't clothe yourself in trout skins," objected Andor, "and when the glacier blows his winds through the trees, it gets too cold to go naked. Down here—" he swung his arm toward the south—"lie the plains, and on their edges in the thin trees, live wolves and foxes and cats. If we want to eat meat and wear fur, we must go there."

"That's true," said Kelan. "I hadn't thought of clothes yet. Let's go that way, then, where the Blue Peaks are."

He referred to an isolated group of mountains, their tops clothed with ragged forests, their slopes stony and inhospitable with thorn. Here centered the vast herds of game, that drifted to and fro in the valley with the rain and the grass. Here, too, lived the beasts of prey that followed the game.

"We might go to the Red Mountains, to the east," said Andor. There seemed to be such a wealth to choose from that decision was hard. "There are lots of animals there in the spring, when the leaves are still tender."

"I've been there," said Kelan. "I went with my father and little brother. We had a hard trip. For four days we killed no meat, and there were no berries. At last we found some apples, and my father killed a bird that was eating them. The way lies all through forests, but it is very rough, and there aren't many fish."

"What part of the Red Mountains did you see?" asked Andor.

"The part that has the biggest cliffs," was the answer. "The sides of the mountains are covered with thick forests, but the cliffs rise high over the trees. Some of them are as red as blood. On their tops we could see snow. Pigs live there, and we killed a little one, and had to climb trees to get away from the old ones. That was good sport."

"I want to see all of the world, some day," said Andor. "The

Salt Lake, the Fire Mountains, the Ice Mountains where the Old Man sits. But now it would be better, perhaps, to go to the Blue Peaks. In the spring the grass is thick there, and there are many animals. Later, when it is dry at the Blue Peaks, we might go on another trip to the Red Mountains." Unconsciously he caught his breath, and waited tensely for the answer to this bold suggestion.

"All right, we might," said Kelan, carelessly, and Andor breathed again.

In this fashion they decided to set out for the Blue Peaks, across the southern plain. Today Mallorca crowns the summit of those hills, which still rise above the youngest of the seas. But where the boys' village stood, today swing endless depths of blue salt water.

Today Sardinia and Corsica float in their blue seas, where once they looked out over trees and rolling plains. The red cliffs of Corsican Piana, then as now, glowed darkly in the dying sun, but today their reflection lies on burning waters, where before it had fallen unheeded on darkening forest-tops.

Then, as now, the Pyrenees lost their tall summits in the summer clouds, but the great glacier on their shoulders, remnant of the ice that was slowly shrinking back to the north whence it came, has dwindled to scattered patches of snow. Today precipitous streams plunge down their slopes into the Mediterranean's calm, but formerly they joined, and formed a great and quiet river. This river, its banks cool with the shade of willows, ran past the tribe's village, through plains that grew ever drier and hotter, and merged at last into a bitter lake of salt, in a land where no rain came. Of that lake, and of the glistening fields of salt that shone blindingly beneath the tropic sun, no trace remains.

The trip lasted six or seven days, for the boys stopped frequently to hunt. They had good luck, and arrived well-fed and fresh at the spring they had been seeking. Here they were caught in the first storm of the trip. It affected them, however, but little, for it was warm, and they had no need for a fire. While thunder stumbled among the rain-hid hills, Kelan worked on his spearhead, and Andor, his knife finished, lay belly down in the drenched grass near a rabbit burrow, waiting to surprise its occupant when it came out to dry its fur after the rain.

A faint movement in the grass near him attracted his attention, and his searching eyes gradually made out the outlines of a red fox, apparently bent on the same errand. Here was luck. A fox-skin was prized almost as highly as a wolf's, for it was supposed to convey to the wearer some of the fox's qualities of a keen nose and swiftness.

Andor pulled up one leg with infinite caution, and planted the toe firmly on the ground in preparation for a spring. Then, as suddenly as if it had been jerked by a string, the fox sprang to its feet and fled. Andor was puzzled. The wind was right, he knew, for the fox's strong scent was all about him. He knew he had made no noise. The fox must have taken fright at something else. Cautiously he raised himself on his hands and

*Without a sound the wolf bared its fangs and trotted toward
the boy, and Andor rose to meet it, hammer thrown back.*

**38**

39

peered over the grass. Not thirty feet away, ambling carelessly through the rain, its massive head swinging from side to side, came a gray wolf.

They saw one another at the same instant. Andor's heart contracted with terror, and yet with delight. Here was his great chance. Here was the skin that would bring him honor at home, and would place him in the envied ranks of the wolf-killers. Not one boy in ten brought back a wolf skin from his manhood trip. His weapons were good—a longer and heavier hammer than the first, and a flint knife which, while crude, was still sharp and jagged. If he succeeded, his place at home was secure. No more would he be Andor the Little.

But if he failed? Fortunately he had no time to follow this line of thought. Without a sound the wolf bared its fangs and trotted toward the boy, and Andor rose to meet it, hammer thrown back.

At one instant the wolf was on the ground before him, and his hammer, aimed at the chisel-shaped head, was whirling its arc over Andor's shoulder. The next, Andor was on his back, the wicked teeth gripping his shoulder near the neck. With a desperate lunge he slashed the knife upward into the long-haired belly above him. He felt the wolf let go its grip, and quickly rolled over and sprang to his feet.

As if confused by this show of fight, the wolf stood still an instant—long enough for Andor to pick up his hammer. As he stooped and straightened a black dizziness struck his eyes, but he shook his head and cleared them. The wolf advanced a step, hesitatingly, and Andor, wild now with elation, stepped to

**40**

meet it. He was winning! With a yell that woke the echoes of the hills he swung the hammer again.

But the wolf, despite the crashing blow it had taken, was not entirely stunned. It danced nimbly out of reach of the second blow, and again sprang at Andor as the boy was thrown off balance by the swing of his weapon. The teeth ripped Andor's arm before Andor could again slash upward with his knife.

Kelan, warned by Andor's cry, rushed to the rescue. He did not stop to think that the rules of the manhood hunt forbade such help—that Andor must either conquer the wolf himself or be killed by it to avoid disgrace. He only knew that his new-found friend was desperately in need of him. His spear, aimed and thrust with the strength of panic, struck the side of the wolf's throat. The animal wheeled to face him, but Kelan kept the spear-point in the wound, and the wolf's struggles to attack him served only to lacerate its throat the more. Andor, regaining his feet, struck again and again with his hammer—feeble one-handed blows, but enough at length to reduce the wolf's raging attack to uncertain twitchings, and then to silence.

It was done. Andor was a wolf-killer—a great name in the tribe. But was he? Doubt in his heart, he kept silent while Kelan washed his ripped arm and shoulder, and licked his wounds to prevent infection, as the old men had taught them. Then the subject had to come up, for one or the other must skin the wolf, and lay claim to the kill.

Under ordinary circumstances there would have been a fight, the more deadly because each would have felt the necessity of concealing the guilty secret of the assistance that had been given. Yet something had appeared in the boys' relation-

**41**

ship that was far out of the ordinary. Kelan, moved at first simply by a feeling of pity for the tormented Andor, had seen enough of his mind to realize that there was, in Andor, a friend who could be a great thing in his life. Moreover, he could not imagine himself forever seeing in Andor's eyes the reproach that would lie there if he should take advantage of his wounded friend.

Though Andor objected, Kelan carried his point, and to Andor fell the task of skinning the wolf. But he was too weak to hunt, and was forced to sit by the carcass for three days, skinning it, eating some of the meat, and sleeping long hours between. A loathing for it grew so strong in him that he could hardly bring himself, when the hide was finally scraped clean and dried, to hang it over his left shoulder in the proper fashion. But the thought of the honor of it made him do it while Kelan was near, though when he was away he left it off, for it galled his wound.

The wound was not severe, for by good fortune Andor's first blow had broken one side of the wolf's jaw. Otherwise the teeth would have closed on his throat at the first attack.

Kelan hovered over his sick friend, torn between envy, elation, and pity for Andor the Little, wounded and helpless. But his spirits would not long stay down, and the sensation of elation won the day. Envy was ended when Kelan killed a lynx, so that they were both sufficiently clothed. And pity died on the day when Andor, still pale and uncertain of step, nevertheless brought home a freshly-killed rabbit. Elation only was left—partly for his own sacrifice, which must forever remain secret, and partly for the fact that he had been the first to recognize Andor's worth.

**42**

Long noontides, when the baking sun precluded hunting, and moon-washed evenings, when the air grew cool again, the two boys sat and talked. There seemed to be endless subjects, Kelan's light wit filling the gaps in Andor's far-flung thoughts.

"What's over there?" asked Andor, pointing to the farther stretch of plain beyond the Blue Peaks. "Nobody has been there, have they?"

"I don't think so," said Kelan. "At least nobody has come back. They say there are deserts there, and a salt lake bigger than the one our river runs to."

"Let's go some day," said Andor, eagerly.

"And be food for the lions? Or get lost without water? And find no fish?"

"You and your fish!" snorted Andor. "I wonder how you have stood it so long down here, without seeing a trout for half a moon."

"Oh, I don't mind," said Kelan. "I see you every day."

Andor grabbed for Kelan's long hair, and they rolled on the ground in a tangle of arms and legs. In a moment, however, they were quiet again, and Andor's eyes and thoughts were over the intervening hills, ranging the plains beyond. He could not leave the subject.

"Perhaps that is where the ducks go in winter, or perhaps there is a land there where the grass is always green, and the animals stay all year. Perhaps we might persuade the tribe to move there, and find better hunting. Then we could build a new and better village."

"And perhaps not," Kelan smiled. "I can't imagine Talgar

**43**

or old Konor moving to any new village, as long as they rule the old one. Can you?"

"No," said Andor, "but they won't rule it forever."

"Then perhaps you expect to rule it yourself," taunted Kelan.

"Perhaps," said Andor, and was promptly rolled over in another tussle.

Andor's strength was returning like a tide now that the wound was healed. The moon was waning, and showed only a half-open door into those bright spaces behind the sky where the chiefs and great heroes went after death. It was time to begin the homeward journey.

So the two young men started out. Kelan, walking ahead, was lean as an aspen sapling. His long dark hair tumbled over his shoulders, and mingled with the brown fur of the lynx-skin he wore. A girdle of rabbit-skins, forefeet tied to hindfeet, clasped his waist, and supported the light hammer of nephrite he had made. In his left hand, parallel with the ground, he carried his six-foot spear, tipped with black obsidian.

Andor was just as slender but much shorter than his companion. On his arms and legs the muscles showed as long sinewy lines. His smooth face, pale from his illness, was framed in light wavy hair that fell, like Kelan's, to the shoulder, held off the face by a leather thong around the brow. The great wolf-hide hid all his body, even though the legs were looped up and tied around his waist to be out of the way. In his right hand he carried his heavy granite hammer, from which, to his dismay, the wolf-blood stains had

**44**

worn away. Thrust into a fold of the hide was the gray flint knife that he had been chipping when the black man surprised him—it seemed months ago.

In this fashion they came home. The day before they reached the village Kelan added to their glory by surprising and killing a doe, which he carried in and dropped dramatically in front of the chief's hearth.

There ensued such merrymaking that the boys were in danger of losing their heads entirely. But when Andor's mother pressed him close, and begged him to be careful, he forgot that he was now a man, and cried tears of mingled joy and love. The little boys stared at him round-eyed, or touched his red scars with reverent fingers. The girls flushed and paled alternately as he went by. When he remembered that, a short six weeks before, they would not look twice in his direction, he was at a loss to explain the mind of woman.

Stor came home the same day, a wolf-hide across his massive shoulders, and not a scratch on his dark skin. He had not come on the wolf by accident, but had ambushed it, and killed it with the first terrific blow. Andor's comfort was that Stor's wolf-hide was an inch shorter than his. No one questioned whether Andor had had assistance in killing his wolf, and the guilty knowledge gradually ceased to clamor in his mind.

Of the others, only one failed to come home. Little Eltan, more and more nervous as the day of the hunt approached, had apparently slipped off by himself to the south, along the river. He had been seen, once, when the hunt was two weeks old, and had then been squatting by the river, trying to snare fish. After that he disappeared. Whether he had fallen in a fight with some beast, or whether, famished and feeble, he had been tracked and killed by wolves, none knew. Only his mother mourned him deeply. There was no use searching for his body, but his mother, nevertheless, made long trips across the southern plains, returning empty-handed from them all.

But among the others there was rejoicing over their own good fortune—sharpened if anything by Eltan's loss, for it showed something of the dangers they had faced and conquered. In a little while the busy life of the tribe absorbed the new-made men, and the press of the summer's work made memories short.


Andor worked, one day, on his new hammer-head. It was of granite, massive and tough, and smoothing it to receive the shaft gave him some trouble. As he chipped and rubbed it against another stone, he became aware of a little figure watching him intently.

He knew the girl for Bardis, old Bardan's daughter. She was a grave, slender little girl, just thirteen, so that she was not of marriageable age. Her ebony hair all but obscured her face, for only marriageable women were allowed to bind their hair. For this reason also she was naked, although her elders all wore short skirts of soft gazelle-skin. She watched Andor's work without speaking or moving, until she noticed him searching for a fresh tool. Then she picked up a flint and offered it to him. He smiled and took it absently, but it was enough encouragement for her to squat down by his side when he began his work again.

"Why aren't you at home?" he asked suddenly. "I thought you had to help your mother all the time, since your father was hurt."

"I should be, I suppose," she answered, "but I'm tired of nothing but work. I wanted to rest a little. Father is better today, anyway."

"But if you walk around in the woods this way, the blacks will catch you." He spoke playfully, as to a little child, but he began to have an uncomfortable sense that she was something more than that.

The girl smiled shyly at his teasing. They fell silent again, Andor working while she watched, absorbed. Presently she turned to him.

"Why don't you get married like the others?" she asked.

Andor was taken aback. He felt no resentment, however, at her innocent question. "I don't want to," he said. "I don't want to marry any of those girls."

"But don't you want to marry some one, some day?"

"I don't think so," he answered. "I don't care much about it. I'd rather hunt, and explore, and—and—things like that."

"Like what?" Her black eyes were fixed on his face, but his blue ones peered under the trees at the brown plain beyond.

"Oh, something worthwhile. Find a great herd of game, or sing a new and splendid song, or think of a way to keep the blacks away, or—something to make them think me a hero."

"That would be wonderful," she said, softly. "If you could have kept the blacks away a month ago, that time they stole the meat from our house, then my father wouldn't have been hurt fighting them. And then I wouldn't have to do so much work for the people who bring us meat. I'd much rather work just for my own family."

Andor fell silent, but the thought had fallen on fertile ground. The blacks, like jackals following lions, had grown so bold that they often stole meat from the very doorsteps of the village houses. They always fled when attacked, and were only dangerous to children, or when they greatly outnumbered a small hunting party. It was only recently that they had appeared, so that it seemed that the one whom Andor had fought, in the spring, had been one of the forerunners of a considerable invasion.

"If there were a big ring of rocks around the village," said Andor at length, "perhaps it would be easier to keep them out. Or, instead of rocks, a wall of bricks, like the wall of a house."

"But nobody could build such a great wall," objected Bardis. "Just think how big it would have to be—around the whole village. If it takes a whole summer for a man to build a house, it would take him years and years to build a wall like that."

"If everybody helped, it might not take so long. There is lots of time in winter, when there isn't any hunting to be done."

**48**

Bardis said nothing, but her eyes did not leave his face. Embarrassed by the stare, and excited by his idea, Andor jumped to his feet. "That's it," he cried. "I shall explain it to Talgar, and then all the men can work on it during the winter. Very soon we would have a wall that would keep out the blacks, and also the lions and foxes that try to steal our meat."

Bardis, deserted, sighed gently, and watched him as he marched off to the village to find Kelan, and discuss the thought with him. When he was out of sight she picked up the flint he had been using and carried it with her, as she strolled back toward her own house.

Kelan was not impressed by the idea. To him there was more fun in a long exploring trip, or in a nicely planned hunt. But Andor was persistent, and eventually Kelan came to feel himself almost a partner in the enterprise. The old men to whom they spoke of the project were uninterested, and it gradually became clear that Andor's advocacy of the plan made it impossible for the others to accept.

But Talgar, the chief, who was not idly called "the Wise," saw the merit of the idea. Calmly disregarding its authors, he named it Talgar's Wall. This silenced the criticism, and served also to allow people to forget that the scheme had originated with Andor the Little. That winter, whenever a full larder gave a few days' or hours' leisure, the wall grew steadily. By the following spring it was higher than a man's head, and surrounded the village completely, with but two gates that could easily be watched. Although none gave him credit for the plan, Andor could gaze at his wall with swell-

**49**

ing pride, and at least Kelan and Bardis knew that he was justified in calling it his.

As fall merged into winter, and work on the wall was just beginning, the curing of meat, the drying of hides, and the gathering of roots and nuts and apples went on apace. The women searched for fruit and tubers, while the men hunted the remnants of the game herds that melted away as the grass grew brown and sparse. Four or five of the strongest tribesmen would lie flat in the grass, while others tried to maneuver a herd of horses in their direction. Stor, thanks to his wolf-skin, was usually among the hunters, although as a rule the young men did only the beating. When the driving was successful, a hunter would spring to his feet five yards in front of the pounding hoofs, and try to plunge a spear into the horses' strained throats. Often he would miss, for the little ponies, tough and lithe from lives of constant flight from danger, would sometimes dodge the swiftest thrust. At other times an old stallion, leader of the herd, would refuse to flee, and would charge with open mouth and plunging hoofs. It took courage to face the stampede, skill to judge the instant for the throw, and strength to pierce the tough hide and muscle of the victim. Andor, to his chagrin, was kept among the beaters, and never had the chance of bringing down a horse, though Stor, cat-like in grace and speed in spite of his huge size, killed several.

Antelopes and gazelles were easier, for they tended to follow certain paths and could easily be ambushed. When checked they would stand foolishly an instant before taking flight again. Moreover, their hides were less tough, and a

**50**

spear could even be crashed against their ribs with some hope of causing a fatal wound.

The winter for which these preparations went forward was not severe. The game animals largely disappeared, though there were still rabbits and foxes, and occasionally a hungry otter on the river bank. There was no snow, but a succession of cold rains that kept the tribe busy repairing house walls, and gathering dry firewood. The larders were full, however, and save for the building of Talgar's wall, there was little urgent work to do. Consequently it was a season for dances and celebrations, and for long evenings of song about the open hearths. Wrapped in hides against the damp winds from the mountains, they would sit in silent circles about the fire, while Talgar and Iri sang of the old days of the tribe, and the young men whispered the words over to themselves, knowing that they too must sing them some day.

One of the favorite chants dealt with the tribe's trek from the highland caves to their present valley home. This Iri sang, in the indeterminate twilight of one misty winter evening. As he sang he raised and dropped a long hollow log, whose end, thumping the ground, gave out a rhythmic, resonant boom. Accompanied by this monotonous punctuation, and by the low humming of the other old men, his great voice hushed at the age and importance of his song, he chanted:

> "In the year of the bison
> And the day of the leopard

*It took courage to face the stampede, skill to judge the instant
for the throw, and strength to pierce the tough hide and
muscle of the victim.*

Osor went out
From the cave where they dwelt
The cave that was painted
With years and with days
The cave that the north wind
Never could find
The cave that the Old Man
Watched with one eye.
Osor went out
To the fields of the South.
His spear was a tree
Pointed with onyx,
His hammer a cliff
That fell upon wolves.
His feet pressed the grass
Where the horses had fled.
His eyes were a wind
That frightened the birds.
Osor went out
To the fields of the South
And saw the white river
The glacier sent down
And saw the white river
That drew all the game.
Osor went up
To the cave where they dwelt
And spoke to the Old Man
Who watched with one eye.
The old men came down.
The young men came down.
The women came down
And Hastor came down,
Down to the river

That drew all the game.
In the cave that was painted
With years and with days
Live lions and foxes
And lynxes and wolves.
The eye of the Old Man
Looks down on their bones
In the cave that the north wind
Never could find."

When he ceased, the humming gradually died, and the massed rows of people, shaggy with hides, sat silent in the dark.

"Where do you suppose that cave is, Andor?" whispered Kelan, as Andor gazed raptly into the guttering flames.

"I think it is up in the forests of the North," he answered. "Some day I shall go and see."

With the coming of spring and the completion of the wall, Andor's mind grew restless, and he spoke to Kelan of another long trip. "Beyond the Blue Hills," he said, "we could see a long valley leading to the west. You remember, last year, how we thought to explore it, but couldn't because we had to be back in a month. Let's go there this year."

"But why there?" objected Kelan. "It looks hot and dry, and I'm sure game would be scarce. Why not northward, into the cold forests, or eastward to the Red Cliffs?"

"There is something that I'd like to find out about that valley, though," said Andor. "It's not like other countries that we've seen—I don't quite know why. And in the spring there should be plenty of grass and game."

But Talgar, when the young men asked his permission, forbade it. There was too much to do, he said, too many mouths to feed, and too much danger from the encroaching blacks, to allow two strong young hunters to be away so long a time. With rather bad grace they submitted to his ruling, and confined themselves to short excursions into the surrounding plains and woods.

For Andor it was not an unmixed disappointment. Between him and Bardis there had grown during the winter a curious community of feeling. She was now fourteen, and by next year would wear the skirt and the bound hair that would mark her as ready for marriage. This did not seem at first important to Andor. He simply enjoyed being with her, for she made a quiet but appreciative audience to his soliloquies, and accorded him an admiration that subtly flattered him. To her, as to Kelan, he poured out his hopes and ambitions. If she had received them as Kelan did, with good-natured banter and affectionate jest, he would have been deeply hurt. Instead, she remained grave and thoughtful, and yet understanding, so that he was encouraged to go on.

Then, in the late spring, the boys who had achieved manhood chose their brides, and Andor, watching the ceremony, knew now what his feeling for Bardis meant. She was not yet of the right age, but there was no harm in preparing the way for the following year. He spoke to her crippled father, Bardan, whose injuries in the fight with the blacks had left him with a useless arm. Bardan struck the bargain, and Andor, shakily elated over his new relationship to the girl, threw himself unstintingly into the work of the tribe.

Throughout the summer Andor and Kelan, almost inseparable now on their trips, tramped the wide plains and rolling ridges around the village. Talgar's edict kept them from going more than a few days' march away, and always they returned laden with meat for the larder. But to Andor there was an eternal fascination in the valley beyond the Blue Peaks. He spoke of it to others who had ventured into it, and their indifference only heightened his own interest. There was nothing in the region, they said, except rocky hills and grassy plains, with few streams or trees. Beyond that? Well, they hadn't been beyond that, but it was probably just the same.

The summer passed swiftly in these pursuits, and the gray rains of winter were upon them again. This time there was more leisure, for the wall was finished, and held the blacks out of the village. They still were seen often, but beyond frightening a few bands of women and children who were gathering fruit, they were not a menace. Therefore Andor had more time to sit with Bardis in the evenings and build with her fantastic plans for their common future. The love that he felt for her grew all the stronger for its delay, and on her part she worshipped him unrestrainedly. Together they squatted in front of the singing-fires, while the old men chanted about the tribal heroes, and the mists from the

mountains magnified the houses and the wall behind them
into unfamiliar shapes.

"Arran, the Slayer
Of beasts and of men,
Walked in the forests
Walked on the mountains
Seeking the antelope
Driving the deer.
Up from the forests
Raging and roaring
The Bear of the North
Came hunting them also.
Bear and man met there,
Fought there the long day,
Fought 'til the birds
Of the forests were frightened,
Fought 'til the rabbits
Sought their retreats.
When darkness descended
The Bear of the North
Was bleeding and weary
But Arran the Slayer
Of beasts and of men
Was strong as he was
At the flush of the morning.
Down came his spear
To the throat of his enemy.
Deep went his spear
In the bath of his blood.
Home to the cave
Where the forefathers dwelt
Came Arran the Slayer
Of beasts and of men,

Bearing the claws
Of the Bear of the North
To hang on the walls
Of the cave where they dwelt,
The cave that the Old Man
Watched with one eye,
The cave that the north wind
Never could find."

"Some day I'm going to find that cave," said Andor to Bardis, as he had once said it to Kelan.

"Take me?" she asked, and turned her black eyes to his.

There was silence, while the old men muttered among themselves, and Andor and Bardis stared through the cold mists of the valley, toward the shrouded forests that lay beyond. Andor was thinking of the trip, and picture after picture swept before his eyes. Forests, cool with spring rains and murmuring with young leaves—piled boulders on the wooded hills, a doe, her forefeet swept by the waters of a tiny stream, her head up and her huge ears groping for the least sound.

Through Bardis' mind ran also a series of pictures, much like those that were bemusing Andor, but in each of them was Andor's image. Now he was laughingly scaling a wild cherry tree, dropping its fruit into her extended hands. Again he was stalking game, and she could see the back muscles ripple as he crept from shelter to shelter with breathless caution. Or they would be preparing for the night, she clearing a grassy level space for sleep, while he worked on a spearhead, his face warm and intent in the fading light.

"It would be fun, you know," said Bardis.

"We'll do it, then," said Andor.

Throughout the spring Andor, with love in his heartbeats, drove his body furiously through the tasks required before he could marry. In his case this meant building a house. Day by day the mud walls gained height, until the roof beams could be laid. The house was a single room, only about six feet wide, for bigger sticks than this were almost impossible to cut with stone axes, but it was over twenty feet long. Its roof slanted one way, so that the wall which faced the center of the village was only five feet high, and the rear wall over seven. The only opening was a door in the center of the lower wall. It was the full height of the wall, its upper jamb being simply a log laid across the top of the wall to support the roof beams.

A thatch of palm leaves completed the house. The roof occasionally leaked, the walls always needed patching after heavy rains, and the whole structure could only last a few years at best. But the pride with which Bardis watched it grow, and with which Andor led her under the completed roof, could not have been greater if the house had had a window or a hinged door—two inventions that lay centuries in the uncertain future.

When it was done, and when the young men of the year chose their brides, Andor and Bardis were married. For six exquisite days they roamed through the verdure of deep summer forests together, and then returned to their home.

The days grew shorter. Sometimes Andor sat in rapt wonder at the great change that had swept over his life; at others he threw himself feverishly into his tasks, fearing somehow that if he did not do them well his happiness might be taken from him. Two years ago he had been Andor the Little, Stor's butt and one of the village's disregarded gamins. Two swift years had changed him from a child to a man of property and worth, a wolf-killer, and a boon companion of the radiant Kelan. If he was not yet a hero, he felt (in his confident moments) that that acceptance could not be far off. And somehow, in that time, this wife had come to him. She was a never-failing delight. She admired him when his vanity needed it, she encouraged him when he was tired, and she loved him so that there was nothing in the world for her except his wishes. She worked hard without seeming to, and kept their house as clean as any in the village. And yet she could drop her woman's tasks, and sit by his shoulder in the evenings, listening to his still boyish dreams and hopes. Never was there such a wife.

In the spring after their marriage, Andor and Bardis struck northward into the forest. They were seeking no particular end, though they spoke often of the cave of the Old Man. In leisurely fashion they traveled or hunted, for the year was rich with early spring and an abundance of game. Andor taught Bardis much of the skill and patience that the stalk required, so that she learned to lie in wait for rabbits, or to imitate the chatter of a squirrel, and so coax the irritable

62

In the spring after their marriage, Andor and Bardis struck
northward into the forest.

little beast within range of a lightning hammer-blow. Together they found the roost of a covey of black-fowl, and made havoc among the stupid, sleepy birds in the dim moonlight that illuminated them.

Then in the long evenings they would talk—though usually Bardis was only the attentive audience. Just as to Kelan on their boyhood trips, and as to Bardis herself during the time of their courtship, Andor poured out to her now the intangible longings of his mind. Here Bardis was often puzzled. She could understand his desire to become a great hunter; she shared his wish to become a wise and respected counselor of the tribe. But much of Andor's yearnings of ambition seemed to assume that the tribe's present mode of life was inadequate, or that in some way that neither could understand there were perils to be thwarted or great deeds to be done to keep the tribe in safety or to better their condition. And, in her present happiness, she could see no need for changing anything in the world.

Andor she had, and her world needed nothing more to be secure, and supremely happy. He was skillful in the hunt, wise in the lore of the land, gifted with a daring imagination (the wall alone proved that) and would soon be respected among the men. Moreover he seemed, most of the time, to live only for her service. Only at times, when his low voice spoke, almost of itself, of plans and hopes and visions of his future, did she feel him slipping a little from her, drawing a little ahead of her in some chase in which her feet were not swift enough to follow. Then she would try, by little attentions, by teasing, and by soft caresses, to bring him back to familiar ground. And always, in time, she won.

As the young summer grew, a new factor made itself felt. No longer could Bardis keep up in the long trips or the swift chases in which Andor gloried. They turned homeward, therefore, so that Bardis's baby might be born, aided by the wise and ministering hands of the women. During this slow march home Bardis felt a new warmth, a new strength, in her relations with her husband. It was she, this time, whose thoughts outran his, and he who, a little puzzled, tried to pull her back to ground familiar to them both. It touched her to see him groping after her, trying to understand the rapt pleasure in her eyes, but she felt that it forged a new bond between them to have it so, and she was content. For, whenever she felt her child move, though she could not explain it to Andor, she thought of it only as a part of Andor himself, given to her to keep and to nourish. Nothing could part them now.

In due time they came home, and in due time the baby was born. Andor's faintly puzzled incomprehension turned to pure joy, and he neglected even his hunting so that he could be near this miracle that had happened to him. Bardis, watching him with the baby, knew the deepest of contentment.

Throughout the winter Andor was eternally busy, supplying the larder, patching the roof, digging ditches to keep the rain water away from his flimsy walls, and popping in through the door whenever he could to catch a glimpse of his sleeping son. They called the boy Mendi, for Andor's dead father, and they watched each petal of the opening bud

**65**

with all the tranced delight that warm-hearted parents have felt throughout all time.

But when another year warmed into greenness Bardis found that though the boy was a constant delight, he was also a constant care, and if Andor was to take any more long trips it must be without her. Secure in his love, and in his love for the baby, she urged him to do so. On his part he needed little spurring. The inaction of the winter, happy as it had been, left him with muscles eager for use. He fell back upon Kelan for these journeys.

In the years that followed game remained plentiful, and in spite of the toil and privation that were their constant lot, the people prospered. Andor gained little more in stature, but his shoulders grew thicker and his chest deeper. His legs, ridged with smooth muscles, became the swiftest in the tribe, and, because his weight was small, he was tireless on the march.

Bardis matured, too, but still retained her slender, upright figure. Two years after Mendi was born she bore another child, this time a girl, whom by custom they named Andis. The ordeal was almost as much as her slim body could bear, and it was long before she could rise and take up again her own household tasks. Thereafter, two babies proved an even more effective barrier than one to Bardis's adventuring, and Andor hunted only alone or with Kelan.

Together they roamed widely over the valley, that valley now known as the western Mediterranean Sea. They saw the long ranges of the Appenines, terminating in the awesome Fire Mountains. They gingerly approached the deadly salt lake west of Sicily, going just far enough to see that there was no hope there of food or water. They penetrated the valley between the Red Mountains and the gigantic Alps, and swung north and west through the endless forests of France. Always Andor urged that they visit the valley beyond the Blue Peaks, but for one reason or another some other trip had always been decided on.

Whether it was this delay that fired his imagination, or whether it was simply the remembrance of the glimpses he had had of that strange-colored, arid land, Andor did not know. He only was sure that the valley should be explored. It was with an ill-suppressed joy, therefore, that he listened, one spring evening, to Talgar's instructions around the council fire.

"The blacks are really becoming a serious matter," the chief was saying. "In my youth there never were any, or at least so few that we never thought of them. Now we find them actually driving the game off our own hunting grounds, and stealing our kills if we leave them for a few minutes. And now that they've tried to capture children from our village, we can tolerate them no longer.

"Therefore I want four men to travel far to the south and west, to see whence these blacks come, and to devise a way to drive them back where they belong. If there are only these few roving bands that we have seen, we can hunt them down like antelope, and frighten the survivors away. But if there are many more behind them, then we must think, perhaps, of moving to a new country, and building another village that they can't disturb.

"Stor," he said, "I want you and Askar to travel down the river, and around the edges of the salt lake, to see whether they come from that direction. From the lake you can turn to the east, by the country of the Fire Mountains, and come home past the Red Cliffs. The country should all be easy to travel, now, with plenty of game. Andor and Kelan have been to the Fire Mountains, and others before them, but that was before the blacks became so numerous.

"Kelan, you and Andor have made many trips to the southwest. I want you to go that way again, but farther than you have been before. It may well be that the blacks came down the long valley beyond the Blue Hills.

"When you have found the home of the blacks, or the road by which they have come, return to the village and tell us. Don't try to fight them, for they will be too many for you. You are simply going as the eyes and ears of the tribe."

The idea inflamed Andor's imagination. Not only had he been singled out by the chief to go on a trip that was for the service of the tribe, but he was going to the very country he had always longed to see. Kelan shared his delight, and, as the crowd scattered through the village, they locked arms and walked toward Andor's house, chattering of plans. Bardis met them at the door. The news of the new trip, exciting as it was to Andor, struck her with dismay.

"But it will be so long," she cried. "Who knows when you

will get back, or what dangers there are to be faced? Can't Talgar find someone else? Or can't you go a little later?"

"No," said Andor, "he can't—and I can't. This is too great an opportunity to be lost. You wouldn't want your husband to be pointed out as a coward, would you—one who wouldn't take up his fair share of the work of the tribe? And besides, wouldn't you, too, like to know what lies beyond the Blue Hills?"

She was forced to be content, for it was plain that Andor would take no denial. After all, it would only be for two or three months—busy months for her, that would slip by almost unnoticed. She braced herself, therefore, for the separation, and met it bravely.

There were no preparations. Andor, always partial to hammers, took the one on which he had been working when he first talked with Bardis—six years ago. It seemed strange to him that one simple tool of man's devising could live and serve him so long. He had made it when he was barely more than a child, newly graduated to the honors of manhood. He carried it still, now that he was a trusted warrior of the tribe, father of a future warrior.

His knife was new, of red jasper, with a wavy, flaky edge ten inches long. Over his shoulder he wore a narrow band of deerskin, in the loop of which he carried his hammer and two sharp, hard fire-sticks. Kelan carried a heavy spear, and a knife like Andor's.

Within a week they had changed the Blue Peaks from faint outlines on the horizon to hard and perilous slopes under their feet. As they climbed, the panorama of the plains widened around them, losing itself in the violet of the distance. At last they breasted the divide, and saw again that trackless valley leading toward the setting sun.

It seemed an arid land, and yet a closer study showed long green swales along the river bottoms, which must harbor ample herds of game. So wide was the valley where they saw it that the farther slope was invisible, even in the glassy air of the plains.

On they trudged, while the ground beneath them rose almost imperceptibly, and the sides of the valley closed gradually in toward them. By day the sun was like a weight on their shoulders, but at night there was a curious dampness in the air that puzzled Andor—a feeling as of an invisible mist through which the stars peered with less than their accustomed brilliance.

As yet they had seen no blacks. Andor, quick to justify his desire to explore still farther, used this as a reason for going on. Westward and ever westward they tramped, knowing now that none of the tribe had ever trod this ground before them.

After many days they came in sight of two huge rocks, which stood astride the upper end of the valley, a long day's march apart. The valley's floor was getting steeper, its sides more precipitous and nearer together, and ever, through the sunny desert air, they were aware of that curious feeling of a cold mist that could not be seen, but only sensed.

They stopped by the river they had been following, for a noontime drink and rest. The water was faintly bitter, and its taste seemed to add to the indefinably sinister atmosphere of the place.

**70**

"See, Kelan," said Andor, "how the ground rises and the valley narrows as we approach those rocks. That low ground between them must be a pass, leading down to another great valley beyond."

"I believe it is," said Kelan. "I wonder what that other valley looks like."

"And beyond that there is probably another," mused Andor. "I wonder how many valleys like this there are. Perhaps they go on and on forever—just one valley after another. One of them might prove a better home for us than the place the tribe now lives in—a land where the game never goes away, or where there are no cold winter rains. Certainly there don't seem to be many blacks here. What if we found a place like that—do you think the tribe would move there?"

"Hold on," cried Kelan, smiling. "You haven't even seen the next valley yet. You can't start moving the tribe into the one after the next, right away. Besides, this stream is getting smaller, and if we follow it up much farther the poor little thing will dry up completely. I say we camp here, and do some hunting before dark."

Andor blinked himself out of his dream. "If we're going hunting, I see a little herd of gazelles up there that might serve very well."

"Agreed," said Kelan. "Suppose I go to that open space on the stream bank, between the two groups of willows. If you drive them toward the stream they'll probably try to cross there."

"All right," said Andor. "I'll give you a few minutes to get hidden."

Andor circled wide to the left, crouching low and moving smoothly and slowly, while Kelan, hidden by the stream's bank, raced to take up his position. He spent some time studying the folds of the land, trying to guess where he would cross if he were a gazelle fleeing from Andor. Then he picked his spot, and, crawling cautiously up the bank, lay hidden in the grass. A faint breeze blew in his face, and he knew he would not be detected.

Andor completed his half-circle, and rose suddenly over a ridge beyond the grazing animals. They raised their heads to catch his scent, and then with one accord turned and bolted away from him.

Andor didn't know just where Kelan was hidden, and if he had he could not have steered the frantic flight of the little beasts. Heads thrown back, they were springing in immense bounds. They headed for the break in the willows, and closed together as they approached the jump.

Kelan, right in their path, bided his time. He balanced his spear just off the ground and held it ready, for at the speed at which the gazelles were coming he could not hope for a second chance if he missed. When the leader was not twenty feet away he sprang to his feet with one smooth powerful movement. His right arm drew back, and whipped forward. The gazelle could not stop its leap in time, and as the spear point struck its throat it was hardly five feet from the man.

Kelan did not let go of the spear, but with a powerful wrench flung the gazelle to the ground as the spear pulled out. As it fell he leaped upon it, and finished the job with his knife. Andor found him sitting gaily astride the body, starting to cut off a ham.

"One blow, you see," said Kelan. "That's the way I always finish the battle. This meat is very tender, by the way."

"You were lucky," said Andor, falling to work. "If I hadn't driven them in the right place you wouldn't have had a chance. But the blow was a good one. I couldn't have delivered a better one myself."

They slept beside the kill, guarding it from jackals. The night turned cold, in spite of the blaze of the afternoon's sun, and in the air the elusive smell of dampness was more pronounced than before. Twice Andor awoke, sure that he had heard the rumble of a distant storm, but the fickle wind drifted the sound away whenever he strained to hear it.

In the morning each cut off a leg of the little gazelle and carried it with him. It would save at least one day's hunt before it spoiled. Burdened with the meat, they nevertheless made a long march to the westward, and found themselves at sunset passing the northern one of the two huge rocks that guarded the head of the valley. Its gray bulk was covered with patches of grass and mosses, and it seemed to rear its matted head to gaze over the intervening pass to where the red sun sank. A few miles farther there stretched across their path the low watershed that divided them from the mysterious valley beyond.

As they stopped to rest they heard again, this time loud enough to be unmistakable, that dull rumor in the air that Andor had taken for a storm. And yet it was a cloudless sky that darkened gradually above them. As the sun sank the west wind struck chill, and they hastened to find a spring at which to camp. The first one they found was so salty and bitter that it was undrinkable, but farther up the northern slope they found a better one, and slept there.

That night the stars retreated behind a film of cloud, brought up by the west wind, and under the threatening sky the strange sound that they had heard at evening formed a background to their uneasy dreams. When the veiled dawn disclosed the silhouette of the mighty rock they had passed, Andor bestirred himself. He was so near the point from which he could see the new valley that he would not wait to hunt or to scout for blacks before going to view it. Kelan, his high spirits somewhat lowered by the strangeness of the country, went with him. Their long smooth strides carried them over the distance before the daylight was an hour old. As they approached the pass the sinister rumble grew steadily clearer, and the unfamiliar smell and feel of the wind heightened the excitement of the exploration. Unconsciously their pulses quickened and their steps grew wary as they topped the rise.

Across the pass, where they had expected to see a long slope like the one they had ascended, leading down to pleasant lowlands, they saw instead, almost at their very feet, the gray restlessness of the Atlantic Ocean.

Neither spoke, neither moved. The terror that would force them back to safety was balanced by the fas-

D. MOREAU BARRINGER was born in Philadelphia and lives in nearby
Bala-Cynwyd, Pennsylvania. He is a graduate of Princeton University and
was a mining engineer and geologist until he turned to investment counsel
work in the 1930's. Today he is Chairman of the Board of a mutual investment company in Philadelphia and is President of the Meteoritical Society.
He is married with two children, a boy and a girl, aged 10 and 6. As .he
says, his book is based on present day knowledge of the geology and archae-
ology of Europe and upon the character of an individual man, found in all
periods of history, whose life is dominated and governed by a self-imposed
and urgent mission.

cination that pulled them forward. Andor, his mind in tumult with the conflict of his preconceived picture and this strange reality, could not take his eyes from the booming surf, nor force his lips to form a word. Kelan at last broke the silence.

"Let's go away," he said. "Let's run. That water is coming toward us."

"No, I don't think it is," returned Andor. "Only the waves on it are rushing toward the shore. The edge of the water doesn't get any closer."

"But what is it? Is this the end of the land—the end of the world?"

It was, and in their minds there was no question of that fact. Not for an instant did they believe that what they saw was a mere lake, with another shore beyond. The headlands that jutted into the sea, the unending gray sky that slipped unchanged behind the farthest waves, and above all the wind that came out of those unimaginable spaces, wrote End! Andor had wondered how far the world extended, and here was his answer. It was the end of the world, and would remain the end, so far as man knew, for fifteen thousand years.

Gradually the freshness of their terror faded, and Kelan, first to recover himself, realized the necessity of food, and went hunting. He surprised a covey of black-fowl, and killed two. With the huge birds slung over his shoulder, he at length persuaded Andor to come away, to some place less exposed to the searching west wind, and sit with him.

"The hunting here will be good," said Kelan, "and I, for one, am tired of constant traveling. This little cave might

*They saw instead, almost at their very feet, the gray restlessness of the Atlantic Ocean.*

make a good place to camp for a few days. Then we could make a fire, and eat some cooked meat, as we do at home."

"Yes," said Andor, and, as if bemused, followed Kelan to the cave. Kelan gathered wood, and choosing a smooth spot on a drift-log, punched a little hole with his spear, and started to spin his fire-stick in it. Andor watched him in silence. Neither of them had suggested leaving, for a spell had been laid upon them by their terror. As the day darkened, the thundering surf was less hypnotizing to the eye, but its sound pervaded the air and their thoughts never wholly left it. With Kelan, however, no depression could last forever, and he tried to make light of the paralyzing experience of the morning.

"What's the matter with you, Andor?" asked Kelan. "All day you have stood and stared at that water as if it were the first you had ever seen. You haven't said a word all day, and if I hadn't killed that hen you wouldn't have had anything to eat. Are you sick?"

"No," said Andor, slowly. "I'm not sick." He paused, and his brow contracted in the struggle with his inadequate tongue. He said, suddenly, "I do not like that water. It shouldn't be there. I don't know why it is wrong, but it is wrong." He lapsed again into his studying silence.

Kelan stared. "Now I know you are sick," he said. "Wrong? How can it be wrong? The water just is, and it can't be wrong or right. You wouldn't say a mountain was wrong, or that it was in the wrong place, or that it would be better here or there. A river isn't wrong, it only runs in the place where it runs, that's all. So with this water. It just is. It isn't wrong."

Andor shook his head. He could not explain, he could not visualize, he could not name, the vague but oppressive unease that the ocean caused him. He only knew it was so.

The fear of the unknown lifted by degrees from Kelan's mind, and he found the seashore a new land of adventure. The shore birds were totally unafraid of him, and he killed several, but disliked their unfamiliar taste. He watched them digging clams and mussels, and, imitating them, found new and interesting foods. Andor was lured into the same pursuits, and the sinister atmosphere of the place oppressed them less. Their fire was successful and easy to maintain. Game remained plentiful, so unaccustomed to man that hunting was easy.

In time, as their preoccupation with the ocean decreased, they remembered their mission. No sign of blacks had they seen, so that it seemed obvious that the migration had not come from the south by this route. Hence the scouts should have turned back, and searched for them along the southern edge of the valley they had ascended. But the fascination of the sea still held them from day to day, as summer ripened into autumn.

Andor was returning empty-handed from a short hunt, several days after their arrival, when he happened to cross the same low watershed from which they had first faced the sea. He stopped and gazed again, now to the east, and now to the west. Eastward lay the immense valley they had left. So vast was its extent that from his vantage Andor could see but the smallest fraction of it, falling step by step from the heights of the two great sentinel rocks. Beyond that distant horizon lay all the world about which his life had been spun. It was a green and human land. Laughing rivers traversed it, and it held all the variations of mountain and plain, desert and swamp. On its great levels the warm winds had free play, and in its lowlands the mist rose white beneath the moon. Grass and water and game were abundant, and life was rich. In its heart lay the tiny village, and Bardis and his children were there.

But to the west, close at hand, hardly fifty feet lower than the crest whereon he stood, swung the interminable sea. Its white teeth gnawed at the rocks that held it back. Over its waves strode a wind that smelled of salt and seaweed and gray wave-tossed timbers. Gulls screamed in the air above it, and leaping fish drew silver out of its blue. Despite the radiant sun, the sea was cold, strange, deadly.

Gradually the dreadful truth was born of the labor of Andor's mind. This sea, with its absence of all that supported the life he knew, was a deadly threat to all that he held dear. The water was higher than the valley. And water runs downhill.

The thought grew clear in his mind, and seared it with a scar it would bear forever. Smarting under the invisible wound, driven to action by the insupportable burden of that knowledge, Andor went over his reasoning, unnecessarily and clumsily. There could be no doubt about its truth.

He looked at the frail dam that held back that world of water, and was chilled at what he saw. It was low, fragile, insignificant, a grass string to hold a wolf in check. Might not the water rise in a night and overwhelm it? Impatient for tangible action, he tried at once to find out. He thrust a stick into the water's edge, in a quiet eddy undisturbed by the tumultuous waves. Steadily, incredibly, the water rose and covered it. Andor watched it until it was completely under water, and then raced to find Kelan.

Kelan was of course unconvinced. "How could the water run into the valley?" he asked, as one who explains things to a child. "It can't come up this slope. See, none of it runs this way. It all falls back when the waves throw it up."

"But it is rising, nevertheless," insisted Andor, and he showed Kelan the stick, now submerged a hand's breadth. "It will rise and rise until it runs over the dam, and it will drown all the tribe, and all the land we know."

Kelan grew grave, as the possibility was borne in upon him. "We should run and warn them," he said.

"We could never reach them," answered Andor, slowly. "No, we cannot help them. See how it rises." They thrust another stick into the sand, for the first was too far out to be seen plainly.

A dark sense of helplessness and horror kept them staring at the rising water, though their bodies cried for action— any action, however useless. They sat silent, for there was nothing to be said. Behind them the unchanged hills were bathed in the warmth of the unchanged sun. The ceaseless surf boomed on the rocks as it had always done. The same gulls dipped and rose in the unvarying sea wind. Nothing was altered, and yet to their awestruck minds nothing would ever be the same.

The sun moved westward over the water, and its reflection

glanced in their eyes from a million ripples. Kelan shaded his face with his hand, and gazed fascinated at the ocean's edge.

"See, Andor, see!" he cried. "It has stopped!"

Incredulous, yet aching to believe, Andor stared at the stick they had planted. It was true. The water no longer rose. A little dark space of wet wood stood out above the surface. After another breathless half-hour they were sure. The water was receding.

His mind buoyant from the lifted load, Kelan was radiant that evening, but Andor was still silent and oppressed. The blow had struck too deep in his mind to be shrugged off in a happy mood. He stared at the whispering flames of red and purple that played through the driftwood. His spirit had been the plaything of terror; it was tired.


Day after day they stayed, though Kelan more than once suggested that they resume their search for the blacks. Andor was held fascinated by the scene of his terror, and enough of the shadow had fallen on Kelan to make his arguments unconvincing. They watched and learned to know the daily breathing of the sea, so that a rising tide no longer struck them with panic. But they learned, too, of the ocean's might.

The steady west wind died, and was succeeded by a poignant calm, while the horizon darkened with foreboding. Then the wind tugged at their sheltered fire, and hail swept the ground with the rattle of a myriad hoofs. Rain followed, rain that drew a gray curtain around their cave's door, and ran in a thousand streams over the soil. The whole hillside appeared alive, the bushes whipping the wind stiffly, the rocks and gravel shifting under the sliding water.

Angered by the wind, the gray rollers rose high, and threw themselves, one after another, in fury on the shore. Andor watched them, hour by hour, while the wind snatched at his hair and beard, and the rain pelted his eyes. Storms on land he knew, but never before had he seen such unleashed power as pounded the cliffs in those appalling breakers.

"Kelan!" he called, and his companion, unmindful as he of rain, came to his side. "Watch those rocks," shouted Andor above the din, "there, by the lowest part of the divide. It seems to me they're breaking and washing away in the waves."

Kelan kept silence, shielding his eyes with a dripping hand. Mingled with sheeted rain the salt spume was flung over the men, and the taste of it was in their mouths. The unwearied sea, again and again, swung back from the rocks, and turned and fell upon them with thunder that the wind could not overwhelm. Andor saw Kelan grow still and rigid as he watched the breakers.

"Yes," he said at last. "I believe you are right. The waves have broken some of the rocks." His voice was solemn, and the wind tossed his words so that they were difficult to hear.

"Then the dam will break, Kelan, and the water will come into the valley after all. Do you remember," he turned nervously to his companion, "the spring we found, the night before we came here? It was salty—just as salty as the great water is. Perhaps it was the same."

"What do you mean?" asked Kelan.

"Perhaps the water is already running through the dam, as a stream runs through an old otter's burrow. It will wear it way from beneath, and the storms will break it away from above. It will surely come into the valley."

"Yes, surely," echoed the other.

With nightfall the storm abated, and, seen in the cooled morning, the damage did not look great. Here a rock they remembered had been cracked; there a heap of boulders had been overthrown. Quiet and smiling beneath the blue sky, the ocean rested for its next attack. After that there would be another, and another, and another. How many more would the dam support? They could only guess.

"We must go home," said Andor, "and warn the tribe to go out of the valley, to the mountains where the water cannot flow. If we start immediately we may not be too late."

Kelan agreed. With a long look backward at the recumbent sea, swaying idly under the immaculate sky, they struck out. Down the long slope that led them back to the country they knew, the country they loved, the doomed country, they swung into their stride. They halted a moment at the salt spring, and imagined it was larger than it had been before. It tasted just like the sea.

On they trudged, without a pause for hunting. Occasionally Kelan glanced back at Andor, a new reverence in his attitude. Andor the Little had foreseen this flood, where Kelan would have fled the place in fear, and never have returned to study and define the menace that it held. It was Andor's mind that was going to save the people from a death which the strongest arm or the swiftest foot would be powerless to deflect. Andor had therefore a strength that was of greater service to the people than the strength of Stor, or the speed and skill of the legendary heroes. His heart was glad that it was his friend, Andor the Little, who had this wonderful power.

Andor remained silent, only half observing his steps. He watched the sides of the broad valley as they descended, and tried to visualize the sea covering it. It gave the whole scene an unreality, a sense of futility, that troubled him. So must Copernicus have felt, straightening his back from his littered calculations, when he stamped the broad earth and knew it for nothing but an impermanent atom spinning in the void. Andor would not have understood, had he been told that his vision, like that of Copernicus, was one of those enormous mental leaps that great men were to make, here and there, all through the shining future of the race. He only knew that he was host to a great thought, whose overpowering majesty thrilled him as much as its threat to his loved ones frightened him. At times he could only regard it impersonally. At others he could think only of dark-eyed Bardis, of little Mendi, and the baby Andis. Would there be time to warn them before the dam gave way?

Once a different thought obtruded itself darkly into Andor's mind. What had the tribe ever done for him? Why, then, should he warn them? His mother was dead—he had no one, except for Bardis and their children, and Kelan, about whom it mattered. Why not, then, take his own family, and flee with them and Kelan to the mountains, never to return?

But the thought would not stay, nor would its answer stay either—the answer that this was his greatest chance to show how his mind could help the people more than Stor's muscles. The only thought that remained was the horror of the water, and the necessity for haste.

Fear stretching their strides, they made great progress down the stream. They neglected their usual careful hunting and traveled for four days on the meat of a single doe they had managed to surprise. They were lean and hard, and the muscles rose and fell like taut wires in their legs as they walked. The summer sun was merciless above, and the graveled plain was just as cruel under foot. Hunger walked with them most of the way.

Following the river, they were forced to scale a high bluff overhanging it. Without warning they came in sight of Stor and Askar, who had returned from their own trip and had been sent forth again to find what was delaying Kelan and Andor. Without waiting for a greeting Andor poured forth his story—confusedly and unintelligibly, while Kelan tried to stem the excited flow of words enough to let their listeners understand. Stor listened, at first amused, and then contemptuous.

"So," he said. "So this is your tale. You would bring home this ridiculous story to get yourself a place of glory in the tribe, since you can't win it by strength and courage. It's about what one would expect of you."

"Don't you understand?" cried Andor. "This water will drown us all if we don't get away in time. We have to hurry or we'll be too late."

"Andor is right, Stor," added Kelan. "We have to hurry, and you must come with us and help the people get ready to move."

Stor grew angry. "You're in it, too, are you? Well, I'll see to it that you two don't get to Talgar with any such absurd notions. What about your task? What about the black men you were supposed to find? Did you forget your duties in cooking up this plot of yours?"

Kelan, serious for once, faced up to him. "Stor," he said, "I don't care whether your thick head can understand what we say, or whether you think we are playing someone false. I do know that this message must get to the tribe as soon as possible, and I'll see that you don't prevent it."

"That's what I expected to hear," exulted Stor. "Askar," he called to the fourth man, who had said nothing so far, content to let Stor do all the talking, "you take little Andor, and I'll take Kelan. We'll give them a good licking to make them forget their lies."

There was nothing to do but fight. As Askar closed in upon him, Andor saw Kelan advance cautiously on Stor, spear drawn back, while Stor, dangerously near the edge of the bluff, swung his deadly hammer lightly in front of him. Then Askar attacked, and Andor's hands were full.

Askar was heavy and strong, and Andor, no match for him in a battle of muscles, had to rely on his quicker foot and greater endurance. He danced lightly away from Askar,

*Then Askar attacked, and Andor's hands were full.*

89

and jabbed at him with his hammer. Askar was soon puffing loudly. Each time he paused, Andor jabbed and punched at him with the hammer, staying nimbly out of reach of Askar's clumsy thrusts. A sudden blow smashed Askar's finger against his own hammer shaft, a second numbed his unguarded arm, and a third, hitting his shoulder with stunning force, ended the battle, and put Askar into complete and undignified rout.

Andor now turned to watch the other fight. Stor and Kelan were on the ground. Even as Andor looked, Stor gained his feet, trying to wrench the spear from Kelan's grasp. In a flash Andor saw again the picture of six years ago, when Andor had lain, so, on the ground under the wolf, and Kelan had run to the rescue. Here was his chance to pay back that debt. With hammer thrown back he ran at Stor.

But the short wrestle for the spear suddenly took a different turn. Instead of pulling on the spear shaft, Stor quickly reversed and thrust it downward at Kelan's prostrate body. Kelan's hands were still on it, and his own pull on the spear served to add weight to the stroke. He managed to deflect it somewhat, and instead of his stomach the point struck his thigh. It was a wicked point, of glistening black obsidian, smooth and keen-edged. Andor saw it sink into the smooth skin of the inner thigh, saw the gush of blood that followed as Stor pulled it out.

With the blow Stor dropped the weapon and ran, or Andor would have been upon him. Instead of pursuing, Andor knelt quickly by the side of Kelan, who, propped on one elbow, clutched his hand over a spreading flow of blood on his leg.

**90**

The pain from his wound had not yet made itself felt, and he was puzzled and annoyed at the lassitude that held him prone.

"Did he hurt me much?" he asked.

"I don't think so," Andor lied, haltingly. He tried to stem the spurting blood-flow with his strip of deerskin, with leaves and grass, with his hands. Nothing helped, and Kelan's warm life was running out into the hungry sand.

Then Kelan spoke, and his voice had fallen to a husky whisper. "I am dying, Andor," he said.

Andor clamped his teeth on an indrawn sob. "You aren't, you aren't," he choked. "The wound isn't bad. You can get over it. The wolf did more to me than this, and I recovered!" And all the while the crimson rivulets throbbed out between his fingers.

"I am dying," repeated Kelan, as if he had not heard, "and you must go alone to warn the tribe about the flood. No matter what they say about you, or how much they disbelieve you, you must make them go away to safety. Will you do it?" The first wave of pain engulfed him, and he stiffened to resist it.

"Yes," said Andor, beaten.

Kelan turned his face to the west, where beyond the horizon he seemed to see again the two great rocks, guarding their secret in silence. Then, with the failing of the western light, he died.

All night Andor sat by the body of his friend, and the black plain about him was no more desolate than his heart. He tried to picture the glorious days of their friendship, but the only vision that danced before his blurring eyes was his own hand pressed against the wound, and the red streams that burst around and covered it. At intervals he dozed, but a guilty fear that he was neglecting something would wake him with a start, and the knowledge would come over him afresh, as poignant each time as the first, that his friend was dead. Self-accusingly, he envisioned a hundred ways in which the accident might have been avoided—in which he might have fought both Stor and Askar, or warned Kelan, or come more swiftly to the rescue. But each time the awful finality of death cut his fancying short. Hour by hour the western stars declined and the eastern stars climbed higher; hour by hour the endless night crept on; until at last the wind and the blanching sky told him it was over. Day and its duties bade night and its sorrows be gone.

Andor could not bury his friend as they would have done at home. He had not even a supply of food to lay beside him, to keep him from hunger when he waked from his great sleep. But he managed to pile rocks about the body to protect it from the wolves, and disregarding his own insistent hunger, he stalked and killed a hare, and laid its little warm body beside the cold one of his friend.

Then he set out for home. The trip was never sharp in his memory, and he must have neglected his own hunting badly, for he reached the village nearly dead of hunger and weariness. Little Mendi saw him approaching the house supported by two men, and his cries brought Bardis to the door.

"Andor," she whispered, and the weeks of loneliness that that word revealed were a reproach to her husband, ill as he was. He laid a hesitant arm about her shoulders, and they entered the house.

"Kelan is dead," were Andor's first words. "Stor killed him." He stopped, with a strange sense that there was something else he was to have said, but Bardis interrupted his tired thoughts with her questions. As she alternately wept over Kelan and prepared tender meat for Andor, the memory gradually returned to him. The flood! How could he have forgotten it?

"Bardis," he said, and she looked at him in surprise at the solemnity of his tone. "I must go to see Talgar and the old men right away. Come with me."

"Why must you hurry so?" she asked. "You haven't eaten all your meat, and you are very tired. Soon it will be dark, and we shall sleep. Tomorrow you can see Talgar."

Andor smiled lovingly on his wife. He was with her again, home to her soft arms and quiet voice, home to her veiled eyes and loving lips. But that must wait. "No," he said, "we must go now. You will know why when you hear me."

So they went. Mendi toddled after them round-eyed, and the baby looked out silently from her otter-skin cradle, rocking on her mother's slender back.

Talgar met them at the door of his house—a new Talgar, stern of face and quiet of manner. He bade them enter.

Andor, as if not noticing the chief's demeanor, burst at once into his message.

"We must go away from the village, Talgar. In a little while, perhaps a very little while, the water from a very great lake will come and cover it all, as the river covers the reed-banks in the spring. We must go to the mountains—."

Here Talgar intervened. "What is this, Andor? You say nothing of your errand—nothing of the blacks you were sent to find, and nothing of your companion's injuries. What is this talk about water?"

Andor recovered his breath, and gathered his suddenly disturbed thoughts. Of course—Stor had been here before him, had undoubtedly given his version of the encounter to Talgar, so that his own task would be the uphill one of first persuading Talgar that Stor's recital was wrong, and then convincing him of their peril.

"Kelan is dead," he said at last. "Stor killed him in a fight. I left him on a hill above the western river, and came home alone."

"Dead? Stor told me he had simply hurt his leg in a fight—that you and he had attacked them when they would not believe some tale you told about a lake. He said you had made up the tale because you hadn't completed your errand of scouting for blacks."

"No—no—that's not true." Andor was striving for self-control and calm, without which he knew he was lost. "Let me tell the whole story, from the beginning.

"We found no blacks at all. We scouted along the whole valley of the western river, and saw none. But we came to the end of the western valley—high up at its head, where stand two great rocks on either side of the valley.

"Talgar, beyond the western valley the world ends. There is nothing there but water—salt water, that cannot be drunk. That water is higher than this valley, and in a little while, perhaps a very little while, it will run down and cover all this land, as the reed banks are covered in the spring. Only the high mountains will be safe, and we must all go there.

"When we had seen this, and were hurrying home to warn the people, we met Stor and Askar. They did not believe our story, and fought with us. Kelan was cut in the leg, here, so that his blood all ran out of him, and he died. Stor went away before he died.

"For this Stor should be sent away into the forest for a long time, as we do with all murderers. But first, Talgar, we must flee to the high mountains, to escape the coming floods."

Talgar said nothing, his eyes eyes intent on Andor's ravaged face. Bardis listened in rapt silence. Andor went on.

"Beyond the two rocks, at the head of the western valley, there is a pass, that should lead to another great valley beyond. But in that other valley—in fact, in all the world beyond that pass, there is nothing but salt water. The dam that holds it back is weak, and when the water grows angry it tears at the dam to destroy it. When the dam is broken the water will come into our valley, and devour that as it has devoured the other."

Still Talgar held his peace. Andor watched him to see enlightenment clear the wide brow, to see decision replace study in the deep-set eyes. He saw nothing. Perhaps a repetition of his story might clarify it. "The great water to the west," he said, "is so wide that no one can see the other side. It is so deep that the bottom can never be reached. When it runs over the dam it will fill all this valley, from the Blue Peaks over to the Fire Mountains. No living creature can escape it. Here, where we stand, there will be water higher than the treetops, higher even than these hills. The only way we can escape it is by fleeing to the Ice Mountains in the west, or to the heights of the Red Cliffs, where the water cannot reach. Do you—do you see what I mean?" He spoke respectfully, slowly, as one should address the wisest of the tribe, but within him his patience was strained.

"No," said Talgar, and Andor grew cold at the word. "No, I do not. You say this water is in another valley than ours. How then can it climb the mountains and come into ours?"

"It does not have to," answered Andor, striving to pick his words coolly. "It has already climbed up almost to the top of the dam. Some day it will break down that dam and flow down into our valley."

Bardis sat still in the darkening hut, her eyes warm on her husband. She knew he was right, she sensed the conflict he faced, and she tried hard to understand and help him. It was so far away, so foreign.

Talgar spoke again, and the sound of his own voice gave him confidence. "How can you expect it to fill this valley? The river at our feet does not fill it, but flows far off to the Salt Lake. So would your water do, if it came here. It would not stay, it would simply flow off to the Salt Lake, like the river."

Andor's hands made helpless gestures. It was so clear, so

urgent, so unanswerable in his own mind. How was it possible that Talgar the Wise would not see it? Of course the sea would not flow off down the stream. One had only to look and see how it covered the world beyond the pass to know without doubt how it would fill this valley. But how to make Talgar see it? He tried again.

"It is far, far bigger than this river, or even the Salt Lake," he said. "The waves on it are higher than a mammoth's back, and strike the rocks like a rhinoceros charging. You can see how it would fill this valley, once you see its great size. The wind that comes from it is like the wind over the southern plains, that has not been hindered by a mountain for many days' walk. It is big enough to fill all this valley in a day when it comes."

Talgar gravely shook his head, and his eyes avoided the intense face before him.

"Your father, Andor," he said, "and your father's father, and all the old men of the tribe, have dwelt in this valley since the days of Osor the Finder. Would they have chosen it, and left their deep caves in the mountains to live in it, if it was going to be filled with salt water? Do you not think they knew that they had chosen wisely and well—a place where their children might rear children of their own in safety and plenty? Do you think that the sight of a lake of salt water, many days' march away, should frighten us away from the hunting grounds they have chosen for us?"

"But—but," stammered Andor, "they did not know this water. I have seen it. I know it is coming here, and if we stay we shall all be drowned. I know it. I can show it to you."

"No," said the old man. "My legs will not run like yours, and my spear will no longer fly hard and true like yours. I cannot go to see your salt water. But when the body fails the mind matures. I believe that you have brought this story only for the safety of the tribe, and I honor you for it. But I know also that the wiser and older heads must restrain the rush of youth, and the wise counsel says we should stay here."

Andor looked around him despairingly. How could he combat such an argument? It was so reasonable, and so wrong. His eyes met those of Bardis, and he drew courage from her lifted smile.

"Talgar," he said, "do this for me. Call the old men together, and the young hunters. Let me tell them my story again. Let them send other men to see, young men to whom the trip is not hard. Let them return and say whether or not I speak the truth."

Talgar remained silent, and the only sound in the cabin was the ringing of the crickets in the gathering dusk. Andor held his breath, and from the corner of his eye saw Bardis nod encouragement. Then Talgar spoke.

"I shall do what you ask, Andor," he said. "But I foresee that all wise men will answer as I have done. I shall not advise sending any more hunters to see your water, lest they be lost to us as Kelan was lost. We cannot spare many such as he."

The words struck down all Andor's pride of discovery, and all his fierce urge to carry his point. The dead face of Kelan swam before his eyes. He bowed his head respectfully to

Talgar, and rose to go. Bardis rose with him. Talgar's voice stopped them.

"Tomorrow you shall speak to the old men," he said, "and tell them what you have told me. Tomorrow, also, you will tell us how you have fulfilled your errand, and how Kelan came by his death. Then we shall hear Stor and say whether he shall be sent into the forest. Good night."

Through the shadowless twilight they sought their own house. About them the business of the village ceased, and people withdrew to their doorways. The crickets shrilled distantly. The wind fell to a breath. Night was at hand. In Andor's heart discouragement and sorrow held sway. At his door he paused to look around, but Bardis drew him in.

"Andor," she said, "I understand. Tomorrow we shall make them all understand, too. Come in and rest."

True to his word, Talgar summoned the tribe to council the following evening.

After the meat had been eaten, and the sun had burned a crimson trail down the sky, the people gathered in the dusk before the wall of the bachelors' house. The seven old men, Talgar in their midst, Konor and Iri on his right and left, sat facing the others. Before them sat the men and boys, and in the background the women shifted and whispered. The newly-fed fire crackled and guttered, and the shadows danced on the wall behind the motionless old men.

Talgar spoke. "I have called the tribe together," he said, "to announce and to mourn the death of Kelan. As you have all heard, he was killed by Stor in a fight. Whether Stor committed a murder or not we must later decide. First we must sing the death-song for Kelan. Andor was with him when he died, but could not stop the flow of blood. He was forced to bury Kelan the Merry where he died, and could not sing the death-song over his body. So we must do that for him now."

The announcement caused no stir, for the news had long since gone the rounds of the village. All remained silent, while Iri and Konor. the former thumping the ground with his hollow singing-stick, began the chant.

"Kelan the Merry
Is dead—is dead.
Kelan the Merry
Lies cold and still.
His spear from the hunting
His foot from the chase
His voice from the forest
Are gone—are gone.
Old Man with one eye
Watching the caves
Shaking the snow-clouds
Beating the thunder
Watch for Kelan.
Kelan the Merry
Is coming to you.
Kelan has food
To last him the journey.

Kelan's long spear
Will find you the game.
Kelan's wise counsel
Will guide and enlighten
The tribes of the mountains
The tribes of the dead.
We who are living
Must all follow Kelan
Sooner or later
Must all follow Kelan
Forth to the lands
Of the tribes of the mountains
Forth to the lands
Of the tribes of the dead.
Kelan will greet us
There with the old men
Who went before.
There where the Old Man
Shakes the snow-clouds
Beats the thunder
High in the mountains
Kelan will meet us
Kelan will greet us
When we, like Kelan,
Are dead . . . are dead."

The low-voiced chant sank to silence. Two men brought
the apples and the meat, wrapped in rabbit-skins, that
should have been buried with the dead, but which must now
be buried in the cemetery, where Kelan's spirit would search
for them before starting his journey. Talgar opened the skins
to look at the food, and signed to the men his approval. Then
he spoke again.

"Kelan the Merry will now begin his journey. He was a young man, and had no chance in his brief life to become a hero of the tribe. Therefore he must reach the village of the dead by the long, hard trip up the mountain, and there he must wait until the clouds cover the peaks, and conceal from all but him the open door into the sky. But if he had lived to old age, his skill was so great and his mind so quick, that he might well have become a hero, and entered heaven through the round silver moon-door, which opens and closes in the sky to admit the spirits of heroes. We must mourn his loss all the more that he died before his life was complete."

He paused, and in the silence the soft weeping of the women could be heard. The men remained still, facing stonily ahead.

"And now," resumed Talgar, "we have done all we can do. Let us take up our work again, so that winter will not find us unprepared. But we shall all remember Kelan the Merry, and sorrow for his death."

The murmuring crowd dispersed into the dark. Only the seven old men remained, and a few of the others to whom Talgar called. Andor noticed that these included Kran the Traveler and Mori the Antelope, both of whom were noted for the length of their journeys and their knowledge of the land. Stor and Askar were also included.

To the little circle Talgar spoke, while Andor, as the youngest, brought wood and freshened the fire.

"We have two tasks, my friends. Our first concerns Stor, and the death of Kelan. Two men saw them fight, and one saw Kelan die. Let them tell the story, that we may tell if the fight was a fair one or if Stor is to be sent away to the forest as a murderer. Askar, you tell it first."

Askar, from his seat by the wall, spoke briefly, "Talgar sent us to see if we could find Andor and Kelan. We found them, in the valley of the western river. They had not looked for any blacks, but had amused themselves hunting and exploring. To cover up their fault they had invented a story about a lake that lay on top of a mountain, waiting to run down and drown people. When we said we didn't believe their story, they fought us. Kelan was hurt. After we went away Andor said Kelan died. Andor broke my hand with a lucky blow of his hammer, so I couldn't stay to see. That's all I know."

Although he had expected it, Andor felt his blood rise at this cold and deadly recital. Without waiting for Talgar's invitation, he sprang upright.

"It's not true," he shouted. "They began the fight. Stor began it, and they both ran away when they saw Kelan was badly hurt. Stor murdered Kelan!"

"Is it murder," asked Stor, "when I fought Kelan in self-defense, and when his own hand, pulling the spear away from me, plunged it into his leg?"

"Andor," said Talgar, "did Kelan have his hand on the spear when it struck him?"

"Only to try to ward it off. You couldn't expect him to let Stor stab him without trying to ward it off?"

"But that means that Kelan was armed, too, and was attacking Stor with a weapon. What do you say, old men? Is Stor guilty of murder?"

The old men murmured and shifted their seats, and from their head-wagging a chorus arose, growing stronger with confidence in their opinion.

"No. No. It was a fair fight. Kelan had a weapon, too. It wasn't murder. No. No."

"So be it," said Talgar. "Stor, you are free to come and go. It is very sad that Kelan is dead, but to send our greatest hunter out of the tribe—that would be sad, too. Now, Andor," he continued, "you may tell us your story of the lake that will run over a mountain and drown us if we stay here." He saw a smile flit over several of the grave faces before him. Andor saw it, too. With great effort he spoke calmly.

"It is not a lake, Talgar," he began, "but the water that ends the world. Beyond the Blue Peaks there is a valley, the valley of the western river, which comes down from the highlands in the west. Near its head are two great rocks, that stand on either side of the valley, and are as high and steep as the Red Cliffs toward the rising sun. There is a low pass between the rocks that seems to lead into the next valley, but beyond the pass there is nothing but salt water."

He paused, realizing that his voice had grown hurried and excited. The crowd that had smiled with derision was now still, waiting for his words.

"The water is not simply a lake that fills a valley. It has flooded all the world beyond that pass. Even the mountains are covered by it, and their tops cannot be seen, so deep

**104**

is that water. The wind that comes over it is like the un-checked wind of the plains. The water extends without a break to the north and the south for many days' walk. There is enough, and more than enough, water to fill all the valley in which we live."

The crowd shifted slightly, and kept their silence. Talgar, without a sound, laid new wood on the fire. Andor con-tinued.

"The water fills that other valley nearly to the brink. If it rose only a little, as perhaps it will when the rains begin, it would run over. We found that it rises and sinks a little every day, but not enough, yet, to reach the edge. Some day it may rise enough.

"But there is a greater danger. The dam is weak. Already the water has broken little holes through it, and runs out on this side as salty springs. Those holes will be enlarged like otters' burrows beside the river, until the dam gives way.

"Moreover, the water itself is trying to break the dam down. When the west wind blows, and the Old Man beats his hollow log in the sky, the waves of salt water rise up and break the rocks of the dam. They rush on the shore like bison when the wolves drive them. Some day they will break the dam."

He had his audience now. They were leaning forward, so that the firelight glowed redly on their throats and jaws, and their eyes were in shadow. He hurried on.

"So we must go. I do not know when the dam will break. Perhaps it will go when the autumn rains swell the great water, as they swell our river. Perhaps it will hold for yet another year, or another two years. But some day it will break, and we must not wait for the break before we start.

"I do not know where we should go, but we must find some high ground that the water cannot reach. Perhaps the Red Cliffs will be safe. Perhaps the wide forests of the north would be better. Even the caves of our forefathers may be high enough. But somewhere we must go, and we must go soon."

Held by the spell of his own vision, he stood before them, rigid, a long time after he had ceased speaking. No one broke the silence for a space. Then Talgar spoke.

"You have heard the story brought back by Andor the Wolf-killer," he said. "Do you agree with him about the danger?"

Again a long-drawn silence, then Iri, singer of ballads, spoke in a full but gentle voice.

"It is an interesting story that Andor the Wolf-killer brings back from his journey," he said. "It is a great pity that Kelan could not have come home, too, to tell us the same prophecy."

"Kelan would have told you the same," cried Andor. "We found the water together, and together we came back to warn the tribe. If only we could have told the story to a fair-minded judge, instead of to Stor, there would have been no fight, and Kelan would still be alive. He knew, just as I know, that it is not safe to live here any longer. He made me promise to warn you, and persuade you to flee to safety."

"A great pity," said Iri, as if he had not heard, "but now it is only Andor's word that we must trust, if we are to be warned and flee these terrible waters. What if Andor has not told us correctly? We might perhaps leave our houses for nothing."

Andor could feel the crowd slipping away from his hold, and the knowledge inflamed him.

"Do you say I lie?" he shouted.

Talgar rose quietly and laid a hand on Andor's shoulder. "Softly, softly," he said. "A fight would not win your point, boy."

Here Andor noticed that Stor moved his seat, and slipped into a place behind Iri. He could see that they whispered together, but could not hear them. Talgar's next question, addressed to Mori the Antelope, drew his attention away.

"Swift of foot," said Talgar, "you have hunted the valleys and mountains to the west. Tell us what you know about this lake."

"I have never seen it, Chief of the tribe," replied Mori. "I have hunted the forests that reach up to the Ice Mountains, and have passed south of them into the dry land of rocks and thorns. There is only one desert valley after another there, and game is scarce. But perhaps I have not been to the same place that Andor—and Kelan—saw."

"And you, Kran of the long hunts," continued Talgar, "have you seen this threatening salt water?"

"Many years ago," was the answer, "when I was little more than a boy, I journeyed far to the westward, in company with Astri of the Twisted Hand. Perhaps we, too, did not go just where Andor went. But we saw, from a high mountain ridge, a lake of water, of such great size that the farther shore was invisible. It lay far below us, and the land between was dry and rocky, and empty of game. Therefore we did not go down to the lake. Before we came home Astri was killed by a stallion he had wounded, and I came home alone, as Andor did."

"Did you see the two rocks that guarded the low pass?" asked Andor. "Did you turn southwest from the Blue Peaks, and follow up the slope of the long valley I saw?"

"I do not remember where we went," answered Kran. "I know I did not see the two rocks you speak of."

"Then you were farther north than we were, and on higher ground, above the water. You did not find the low pass where the water can break through."

"No," said Kran. "I saw no such pass. Perhaps we were, as you say, too far north to see it."

"If it exists at all," said Stor.

Attention immediately swung to him, and he raised his great frame lightly from the ground. There was an almost engaging insolence in his speaking now, but he had after all been acquitted of the murder, and was as free as anyone else to express his opinion.

"If it exists at all," he repeated, and paused dramatically. "Yes," he continued, "I believe it does not exist. I believe Andor invented the whole story. In the first place, there is no knowledge of a lake so great that its farther shore cannot be reached, unless a man is too lazy to reach it. I have seen the farther shore of even the great Salt Lake by the Fire Mountains, and so have many others. That is the largest lake in the world, as everybody knows. I do not believe this yarn about a lake, larger than any other, that sits on top of a mountain waiting to run down and drown people."

The circle, as one man, had turned toward Stor, amazed by so much eloquence from him, and attracted by the easier thought. Iri arose as Stor came to a pause and searched for more words.

"It seems strange to me," he said, "that Andor should have found this lake in such a dangerous and hungry country that no one can go there to confirm his story, and that Kran's companion Astri was killed in the same country many years ago."

Andor's wrath was simmering, but Talgar kept him restrained. Instead of letting him answer, Talgar himself spoke.

"Iri," he said, "you have a further thought in your mind. Why do you think Andor would invent so dreadful a tale, if there were no truth in it? What purpose could it serve?"

"Is it not true," answered Iri, "that Andor is anxious to be a hero, and to be admired by the tribe? But to do that one must be a strong man, a skillful hunter. Andor is little and not very strong. Perhaps he sees in this story a way of making himself a hero in spite of his size."

"But Andor is a skillful hunter and a swift runner," answered Talgar. "Remember, he killed both a wolf and a black man on his manhood hunt. Why should he need to invent such a tale?"

"He said he killed a wolf and a black man." Stor was again on his feet. "But none of us saw him do it. Perhaps someone helped him, or perhaps the wolf was sick. He hasn't killed any more, you know, as I have."

Iri interrupted him. "I won't say anything against Andor, and neither should you, Stor. But perhaps it is true that he sees no chance of keeping the admiration of men without accomplishing some new feat.

"For such a reason he might have invented this danger that will devour the village. It would be a very clever scheme. He says that the lake is many days march to the west, in such a difficult country that no one will go and see for himself whether it is there or not. He might hope to get us all to move to a new land, and build a new village. If he did succeed, men might think him as great as Osor the Finder."

"Yes," said Stor. "That would be the only way that men would ever think him so great—only by trickery. Look how little he is."

"Be quiet, Stor," said Iri, severely. "This is no time for such abuse. But think," he continued to the circle, "think how clever such a scheme would be. When his lake did not run down over the old village he could say, 'Beware! Keep away! Some day it will come!' and no one would be able to prove him wrong. Such a man would always remain a hero, for having saved the tribe."

Iri's ending loosened the bridled tongues, and a storm of comment, pro and con, obscured the argument. It was clear, though, that the seeds of disbelief had found fertile soil. Stor pressed his advantage.

**110**

"For this he would want us to give up the strong houses, the good hunting, the clean water, that Osor found for us. Just to raise himself to a seat of honor he would have us all flee to some dark, cold forest of the north, and go through all the unnecessary work of building a new village, in a place far less rich in water and game and warmth than this."

Talgar checked the rising turmoil with a sharp command. "Andor," he said, "was it in your mind to bring honor to yourself by this discovery?"

But Andor's anger was past restraining. He sprang upright, his hand groping for a weapon that was not there. "Stor lies!" he shouted. "He lies in everything he has said. The water is there, and I know it will come into the valley. I never thought of bringing honor to myself, or of trying to be a hero by finding this truth. I wish it were not so. But I cannot keep silence about what I know. And I cannot flee alone with my family to safety, if the tribe remains here to perish. That is the reason I have spoken to you about it. As for Stor, I will fight him here and now to show I am right."

Stor, confident in the knowledge of his strength, laughed. "I won't fight you, Andor," he said. "It would be small honor to be known as the slayer of Andor the Little."

Iri joined in. "I did not say that Andor had invented this tale. I only said it was possible. Andor may have indeed seen such a lake, and may feel a great fear about it. But are we to take flight because of his panic, like a herd of antelope fleeing from a boy with a stick?"

"Not I," said Stor. "I am not afraid of his water, and I intend to stay right here, in the house I built for myself."

*111*

"There will be no fighting," said Talgar. "If you must throw your weapons about, Andor, use them on game for the larder. But you, old men, what should we do about Andor's story? Should we all go to the forests, for fear his flood may catch us? Or should we stay here, believing that Andor is mistaken? Or should we send men to see whether his story is true?"

Stor started to speak, but the gray voice of Konor cut him short. Konor was the oldest man of the tribe. He had never excelled in either wit or strength, and had had to wait until his great age gave him a position of honor. On account of that, however, and his temperate mind, he was listened to with respect. He scratched his few hairs as he spoke, a mannerism everyone knew.

"This is more important than Stor thinks," he drawled. "In all my years I do not remember so strange a story brought back by a hunter. If it is true, we must go to the forests of the north, or the Ice Mountains, to be safe. But Andor is a young man, and at his age men have not the wisdom or the judgment the years bring. Therefore we must not move before others have seen what Andor has seen, and tell us the same story. I say, Talgar, that you should choose a strong hunter, old enough to have a little wisdom, to go with Andor to this lake, and then to tell us what he sees."

"That was well said, Konor. I shall choose a man from among the hunters, a man who has a wife and children, so that he may see the problem as Andor sees it. Such a one will not wish to leave his children to perish in the waters, but neither will he wish to take them needlessly to the hardships of the forest." Talgar stood up, and looked thoughtfully over the faces ranged before him.

"Baltan," he said, "can you go?"

The man he addressed sat in the edge of the crowd. His black beard mingled with the forest of his chest, and his hairy shoulders and arms had earned for him the nickname of the Bear. He was short and massively built, and his pale blue eyes looked strangely out of place in that shaggy countenance. Over his shoulder he wore a rubbed and ragged wolf-skin, for he was among the mighty hunters of the tribe. His thirty winters had sprinkled frost in his black hair, and seamed his face with tiny lines.

"Yes," he answered, "I can start right away. Can you go tomorrow, Andor?"

Andor hesitated. He was very tired, and the mere glimpse he had had of Bardis only whetted his hunger for her. But the stakes that hung upon delay were staggering. Suppose they came too late?

Talgar saved him from the dilemma. "Andor is too weary now. He has only been home one day from his great journey, and his wife and babies await him in his house. Let it be three days before you start."

So it was decided. Three days! thought Andor, threading his way through the dispersing crowd. Where were the long days he had promised himself, stretched beside Bardis in the river-grass, watching over the romps of their children, eating the meat of past hunts? Where the long stillnesses of nights with her, when talk was so useless, and the mere knowledge of the other's presence cast a glory over the mind of each?

Where the leisurely telling of his experiences to an ear that thrilled to the lightest of them? Three days! They would be frittered away in the endless tasks about the house and larder, and he would start on this new trip as if it had merged with the old. He found his doorway, and felt within it the arms of forgetfulness.

"Dearest," said Andor, when the pale sky woke them in the morning. "I must go to the great water again, to prove to the old men that I am right. I am taking Baltan with me. We are to start in three days."

Ice closed around Bardis's heart. "What are you saying, Andor?" she gasped. "You have just arrived home. How can you speak of going again?"

"I must," he answered. "I must show them that I am right, and that we must move to the mountains to avoid the coming flood. They will not believe me alone, so I must take Baltan and show him what I saw. Then perhaps they will know that I spoke the truth."

Bardis wept and pleaded. She showed him their children, and told him how they would not know their father if he stayed away much longer. She used the arguments that unrecorded millions of wives had used before her. Then she fell silent, acknowledging defeat. Within her sore heart was a burning point of pride that he, her husband, who worshipped her above all women, should be the bearer of news so great

**114**

that the tribe must call upon him for such a sacrifice. It was small comfort to her sorrow, but she treasured the jeweled thought.

The three days passed swiftly. Andor was more than ever delighted by his little son. The boy was quiet and obedient, but the boundless energy in those little limbs kept him eternally active. His eyes were roguish and laughing, but they could fix themselves in wonder on vacancy, while their owner probed with questions the fascinating world. To Andor these questions never grew tiresome. He spent hours in little Mendi's company, while they explored the river banks, and the edge of the sweeping plain. From such expeditions Andor would stride home, the child asleep in his arms, and the world to him seemed well-nigh perfect. The shadows cast by Kelan's death and the coming separation were thrust aside—for three short days.

Then the appointed morning came. Their farewell was brief, but for hours it left Andor taciturn and sad. Baltan, never a great talker, swung through the grass in a silence that matched Andor's.

They marched for two days on the provisions they brought with them, and then stopped to hunt for a day. In this way, with a minimum of delay or useless chatter, they covered mile after mile of the graying plains with astonishing speed.

But the hunting grew worse as they went. The August sun had shriveled the grass, and the game herds had drifted east, where the rains fell more reliably. Only scattered and wary bands were seen, and they had to fall back more and more on rabbits. Hunger again became their companion, and followed them as it had followed Andor down the same course a few days before. Baltan, heavy and bulky, began to feel the heat and fatigue sooner than slight Andor. By the time the twin rocks came above the horizon he was dragging behind.

Two feelings fought for mastery in Andor's mind, as he climbed the last ridge that hid from them the terrifying sea. The first was relief from an unspoken fear that the dam might be nearly destroyed, and that this time they might indeed be too late to warn the tribe. The second was doubt as to Baltan. The latter had said practically nothing for several days. Plainly this sort of journey, which required a minimum of brute strength, but a maximum of quiet endurance—and under-standing—was little to his liking. Plainly, also, he was near to staggering with fatigue.

Therefore Andor, uncertain how to introduce Baltan to his first view of the ocean, hung back and let the other cross the divide first. Baltan stiffened with surprise, and instinctively dropped on one knee, as the amazing vista broke upon him. For a long time he gazed silently at the surf, and Andor could see in him the same emotions of surprise and fear that had swept the speech from his and Kelan's lips.

"So this is your great water," said Baltan at last.

"Yes," said Andor.

The stillness of the late afternoon was intense. The ocean's surface, level at a distance, was gently folded near the shore into ridges of waves, that slapped and gurgled about the green-splashed rocks. The sloping sun gilded their crests with dazzling light, which broke into a myriad shards of silver on the shore. Even the gulls, as if unwilling to ruffle the peace of the scene, stood idly on the strips of sand. A smell of sea and sand and patient heat lay upon the earth.

"It's very quiet here," said Baltan.

Andor nodded. He was caught in the mist of contemplation that had enwrapped him here before. He could not say where his thoughts were roaming, nor why they seemed so solemn, so majestic, and yet so enthralling. He hardly listened to the voice at his side.

"Now we're here," Baltan was saying, "what do we have to do?"

Andor roused himself with a start. What were they to do? Why, to look at the sea, of course; to show Baltan how real was their danger. "Look there," he said, pointing to the surf, "do you see how high that water is, and how low is the valley we have left? This is where the flood will break through."

Baltan stared toward the peaceful water before them, and over the valley behind, its deeper wrinkles filling with the transparent evening blue. He said nothing, and Andor, caught in the somnolent magic of the place, lapsed also into silence. Save for the distant whisper of the sea not a sound could be heard. There were no trees to rustle their leaves, and no wind to move them had they been there. Not a living creature, except the two men, and the motionless gulls, could be seen. Far out over the waters the first faint clouds gathered to receive the declining sun. Eastward the bulk of the sentinel rock grew darker, and subtly luminous in the reddening evening. The hypnotic hour still held them fast, while the ocean changed from blue to gold-spun purple, and the sun at last was quenched in its eternal waters, and the hills drew aloof into their mystery of night. Then Baltan roused himself, and together they sought and entered the cave in which Andor and Kelan had camped.

Kelan was very near Andor all that night. Asleep or half awake, Andor could almost see his boyish face, a half-smile on the bearded lips, and yet a sense of deadly seriousness behind the laughter. Then he began to sense reproach in the eyes that looked down on his, and realized how little he had done toward accomplishing his purpose. Somehow he must convince Baltan, now sunk in the heavy sleep of exhaustion, of the seriousness of the case. Tomorrow, perhaps, when Baltan was rested, and the morning sun allowed clearer thinking than this bemusing twilight. Resolved to set about the task with the morrow's light, he fell asleep at last.

They woke late, when the daylight had already washed the shadows from their cave.

"Come," said Andor, "let's go down to the water, and I'll show you how it will break through."

Baltan was in a more cheerful mood now that his strength had been rebuilt in sleep. "Can we eat your water, Andor?" he said. "There is no other food at hand that I know of. It seems to me we'd better do some hunting first."

"You're right," said Andor. The calm water he had seen encouraged him to believe that the danger was not so imminent as he had feared, and obviously Baltan spoke wisdom when he said they must hunt. Accordingly they started toward the nearer of the two springs that lay to the northeast of the divide.

A careful approach and a long look at the surrounding country showed no game of any kind. They walked to the spring, therefore, and drank. Suddenly Baltan pointed excitedly to the damp ground around the water.

"Blacks," he whispered.

On the mud was the clear outline of a human footprint. It was too small to have been made by any white man they knew, and the toes were broad and wide-spaced.

"It's fresh, too," said Andor, examining it. "He must have been here last night. No wonder there's no game. We ought to find out where he went."

A search at the second spring disclosed no further sign of the black, but did reveal a pair of delicate roe-deer. Luck, a good wind, and a stalk of infinite care, brought them so close that when the deer took fright at Baltan they nearly trampled Andor in their first bound. A lightning swing of the hammer dropped the little buck, but the doe fled on twinkling legs across the barrens.

Food was supplied, but the question of the black still loomed large. They could not follow his trail over the rough gravelly surface. They had seen no other sign of him except the footprint at the spring. Yet it was an uneasy feeling that they might have him for a neighbor and that their meat and weapons were not safe as long as he was about. Moreover, there was possibly a more serious meaning than this to the black's presence. Andor and Kelan had seen no blacks whatever on their first trip, although they had gone with the express purpose of finding them. Did the arrival of this one mean that a new migration was coming, increasing the menace that this enemy already offered?

In Andor's mind, however, no thought save of the sea could long dominate. They returned to the pass, and Andor again launched into an explanation of his theory. But the day was calm, and the ocean borrowed the blue of the sky to cover itself with beauty and peace. Baltan was to be excused if he had difficulty scenting danger in that placid air. Ere long he tired of Andor's reiterations, and his wandering eyes testified to his lack of interest.

The dim little fear that had sat in the corner of Andor's mind from the first began to grow. It was beginning to be clear to him that Baltan could not, or would not, understand him at all. Would not? No, it was not that. Baltan's nature was not vindictively stubborn, nor was it small enough to league with Stor against an unpopular new thought. It must be, then, that he could not understand. With no elation, with no vaunting of self, but with a deep sense of loneliness, Andor began to see the width of the gulf that separated such a mind as his from those of his companions.

Bardis understood. But in the clear light in which he now stood, he could see that Bardis took her thoughts ready-made from him, and that she would have believed him no matter what idea he advanced. He was her gospel, and she could never question it.

Kelan? He had known. It had been hard, for a little time, to convince him, but he had seen and understood. But Kelan could not help him now. Kelan could have been a powerful ally in the struggle he foresaw, but, again with a crushing sense of isolation, he knew that even Kelan could not have originated the thought himself. Kelan would gaily have hunted the pass twenty times, and known every rock and tree and trickle of water, but never would he have felt that nameless distrust that the sea impressed upon Andor; never could he have prophesied alone the danger that lay in those infinite waves.

In the sadness of his solitude, only the face of his little son comforted Andor. Here was his hope. Mendi would see eye to eye with him, he knew. Once let that little soft body expand and harden into manhood, and maturity guide that restless mind, and he would have at his side a helper in his unequal fight, a friendly hand stretched out to him through the empty spaces of his loneliness.

It was difficult to shake off the lassitude of these thoughts, and to attend again to the now futile task of persuading Baltan. He tried, but found that Baltan's mind had veered off on an entirely different course.

"That black man," said Baltan, "must have come up from the south, where they all live. We might find him, up near the springs, late this evening. Shall we hunt for him, and see if we can kill him?"

"Why?" Andor was only half attending.

"Well, perhaps not kill him, but at least chase him away. We can't have black men living around our hunting grounds."

"No," said Andor, "we can't. But after all, we only have to look at the water, so that you can go back to the tribe, and tell them I spoke the truth, and that they must flee. It really doesn't matter whether there are black men here or not."

"That's right," Baltan considered his thoughts slowly, and spoke as slowly. "The water is here, as you said, but I don't see how it can ever run down into the valley. Even if it does, how can it ever make more than a river of salt water? It can't flood the whole valley, and it certainly can't come up to the village."

Andor sighed.

"But see how huge it is," he insisted. "It is greater than the valley. It will fill it so deeply that the water over our village will be higher than the trees. You can easily see that. If you want to, we can travel along the shore here, as Kelan and I did, and see how far it extends, but I can tell you now that we shall never find the end of it."

Baltan did not answer. The conflicting ideas in his mind—the ocean on the one hand, the black on the other—rendered him unable to think connectedly on either subject. When at last he spoke, it was of the thought that was more easy for him to visualize.

"I think I'll try to follow the black man," he said. "We can't have black men living on our hunting grounds, lake or no lake."

"All right," said Andor. "I'll help you hunt the black man if you'll try to understand the danger of the flood, and help me persuade the tribe of it."

"Let's hunt him now," answered Baltan, and with that Andor had to be content.

**122**

Content, however, appeared only on the surface. Beneath was a turmoil of dismay, of anger, and of bitter resolve. Clearly his hope of making an ally of Baltan was gone, but not for a moment did he feel that his duty to the tribe had lessened. Only by patient reasoning, and by long planning and expounding, could he hope to accomplish his purpose. But the necessity of accomplishing it was never clearer or more urgent. How long it would take, he could not guess. He could only gaze dumbly at the sea, and hope that it would hold back its destruction until his task was done.

For the moment, then, he must school himself to humor his companion. With Baltan on his side, he could have won his point with ease, but even as a neutral Baltan would be far less harmful to the cause than as an open enemy. Much as it galled his raw nerves, he must nevertheless keep this unwelcome friendship.

"We'll hunt him now," said Andor.

R efreshed by their rest and another meal from the little roebuck, they began their quest, and by some lucky chance it was quickly rewarded. Baltan sighted the distant figure of the black before the hunt was an hour old. He was sitting, oddly enough, almost on the skyline of a low ridge to their right, behind which, Andor knew, was a spring and a little oasis of green grass and trees. Beyond him the bluish bulk of the southern hills stood clear and hard.

"We'll separate," whispered Baltan. "I'll go around behind him, and you appear in front and drive him down to me. I think he'll be easy to catch."

Andor felt uneasy about the curious action of the black, not only in sitting still, but in choosing such an exposed place to rest. But his interest in the subject, dulled by the knowledge of the task that faced him at home, was not sufficient to urge argument.

"All right," he said.

Baltan slipped off to the left, where a series of rocky ravines could conceal his circle. Left alone with the stillness of the hills, lulled by the motionlessness of the air, Andor half watched the distant quarry, half lost himself in reverie.

What a change his discovery was working in his life! This spot—this pass that led only to the world's end—had somehow attracted him from the very first trip of his adolescence. Here he had stood with Kelan, and looked for the first time on the sea, while that strange unease flitted like a bat through the caves of his consciousness. Never, in the months since that time, fraught as they had been with reunion and parting, hardship and love and sorrow, had that shadow ceased to exist. Andor knew that he could never again be free of it, until the flood should come.

The black on the distant hill moved. Andor watched him while he sprang erect, stood for a moment as if listening, and then ran over the hill and disappeared behind it. Evidently Baltan's plan had in some way miscarried. Andor moved forward toward where the black had vanished.

Then he espied Baltan, and waited for him. Baltan, breath-

**124**

less and purple from his run, seized Andor's arm, and together they ran back toward their cave. As they ran, Baltan panted his explanations.

"A whole tribe . . . a whole tribe," he gasped, "camped around the oasis . . . been there a long while . . . pile of bones from their kills. . . . There was another lookout, too. . . . He saw me. . . . They're all excited over it. . . . They may hunt us. . . ."

They reached the cave, and Andor watched the horizon for enemies while Baltan recovered his breath. None appeared, but they held a serious council of war, for war it would certainly be.

"They saw me, all right," said Baltan. "The lookout shouted to the others, and they all jumped up and watched me. Two or three tried to chase me, but I think they lost my trail. I stayed on the rocks coming up that gully; that's probably why they couldn't find my tracks, but they're coming to hunt us, and that's why we've got to get away from here."

"Yes," said Andor, absently. His mind was not on the black tribe. He was thinking with a bitter resignation of the errand on which they had come. What had become of that now? Was it to be forgotten in the excitement of encountering this band of savages, this herd of animals that bore a curious resemblance to men? That would be the final irony.

"Let's go now," said Baltan. "We're rested, and we have to go a long way to find game, with that band of black hunters around. Besides, you can't tell how soon they'll be here."

Still Andor remained absorbed in his thoughts. At last he lifted his eyes to Baltan's.

"Baltan," he said, "if we go now, will you tell the tribe that the flood is coming, and that they must flee to the mountains?"

"How can I?" replied Baltan. "I don't know whether or not it's true."

"You know it's true," said Andor. "In your heart you know it. Never again will you be able to live unconcerned in the village, knowing that in the night the waters may rise around your house. Never will you go for another hunt in the mountains, without the fear that in your absence your wife and children will have been drowned. Never again will you look toward the evening sun, without the knowledge that behind those burning hills wait the cold waters. You do not feel it now, but in the years to come you will feel it, working and resting, sleeping and waking. You will look at your family, and know that the flood may one day devour them. You will light your fire, and think that it may be quenched, not by the rain, but by miles of salt water. You must know it is true, as keenly as I know it."

Baltan said nothing, but ran his thumb over his knifeblade, back and forth, back and forth.

"Look at it!" cried Andor. He stepped a few paces from the cave mouth, to where the view ran unchecked between the handlands that encroached upon the sea. "Look at it. There is more water than our whole valley would hold. And there," he swung his eager arm toward the pass, "is the little barrier of mud and rocks that holds it back. You can see for yourself how weak it is—how narrow, and low—how incapable of withstanding for long the battering of the waves."

Baltan, beside him, stared under wrinkled brows where he pointed. The freshening west wind, coming from the gray sky

**126**

to seaward, was tossing spray over the knees of the rocks below them. The sun was lost in the western clouds, and the hills grew haggard as the light subsided. Baltan shifted uneasily from foot to foot, and shivered a little in the wind.

"We ought to go away now," he said. "Those blacks may be here any minute."

"Wait—look," cried Andor. "Do you see how high the water lies above our valley? Do you see how the ground slopes downward from the pass—downward to the east farther than we can see? Can't you imagine how the waters will pour down that slope, tearing aside rocks and earth and trees? There is nothing to stop them, nothing but that narrow wall of mud. Do you dare leave your friends, your family, in the path of that consuming flood? Will you help me save them?"

Baltan's eyes were on the ground, and his hands betrayed his irresolution. At last he spoke, and his words were low and hurried.

"Let's go home," he said. "I believe you."

"Do you?" Andor wheeled on him. "Do you really? You understand how it will happen—how it must happen?"

"Yes, I understand," answered Baltan. "The water will come over this pass, and flow into the valley." He spoke abstractedly, like a child repeating an uninteresting lesson. Andor disregarded the tone, clutching only at the straw the words offered.

"Will you tell them that at home?" he cried, breathlessly. "Will you help me tell them—persuade them—make them go away and be safe?"

"Yes," said Baltan. Then, after a tiny pause, "Now let's start."

"Let's go, quickly," said Andor.

If Andor's first trip home from the sea, with Kelan, was a hard struggle against heat and hunger, its memory was lost in the nightmare of the second. The blazing sun had killed the last vestige of grass, so that their feet, used though they were to hard marching, were cracked and bruised by endless leagues of bare gravel. They could not hurry, as they had on their upward journey. Not only did their feet slow them, and keep them following the soft ground by the winding river, but they had to spend days in hunting the last remnants of game. Sitting by the tiny hole in the bank that betrayed the home of a field mouse, waiting with marble patience when every nerve cried "Hurry! hurry home!"—that was the most exquisite torture to which Andor had ever been subjected. Baltan was spared the mental refinement of agony, but his physical self suffered more than Andor's. His feet at length became so cracked and bleeding that Andor was forced to hunt for two, at a time when hunting for one was almost as much as he could do.

Lizards and snakes, tiny raw fish from the river, mice, and even insects, made up their famine diet. In the two months of that trip, Baltan's thick body shrank to a shaggy skeleton, and Andor's smooth limbs showed on their surface every bone and joint and sinew. But they arrived at length at the village, their last bit of strength used up in a word of greeting.

Talgar was forced to wait six days before calling the council that was to hear their story. Neither traveler would have been able to stand up, before that, long enough to speak about it. When at last the old man assembled the elders and hunters, Andor's gray face showed a tide of returning life, and Baltan's ribs were a shade less obvious than before, and his eyes a shade less sunken.

As always, the ceremony started with a chant, but since there was no death to be mourned, and no recent deed of valor to be announced, the chant was one of the most ancient—one that had come down, men said, from the cave days on the mountain.

"Popo, the gray man
Popo, whose magic
Kept out the bears
From the cave of the Old Man,
Popo, whose magic
Saw in the forest
The home of the horses
The dance of the deer
Into the darkness
Into the last cave
Went to make magic
Went up to sing.
There with the images
There with the pictures
Of tigers and bison
Of lions and deer
He sang a magic
He danced a magic

**129**

And all of the darkness
Was full of the magic
Was full of the sounds
And the smells of the magic
And all of the caverns
And all of the tunnels
Were full of the magic
Till Popo was done.
Then from the darkness
Into the forest
The bats of the magic
By tens and by hundreds
They carried the magic
That Popo had made.
So the strong hunters
Roaming the forest
Could find many antelope
Hear many horses
Kill many deer.
So to his cave-door
Whining and hungry
Chased by the magic
The Bear of the North
Went without harming
The horses and deer
Went without stealing
The meat of the deer."

As the song ended, the men tore their minds forcibly from
its eerie spell, and saw around them the friendly and familiar
village. It was not hard to visualize, in contrast, the damp
caves, hidden in silent forests and mist-swept snow, that had
seen the birth of that song, in the youth of the tribe. Many

hearts warmed for an instant to the present home, and Andor's urging fell on ears less receptive than if the song had not been sung.

Talgar, squatted against the wall, ruddy with firelight, called on Baltan to tell the story of his trip.

"Tell us, old bear," he said, and men could hear almost apology in his tone for the trials of endurance which he had given Baltan, "tell us of your journey, and what you saw of Andor's lake. First tell us, did you see a lake at all?"

"Oh, yes," answered Baltan. "We saw a lake. There is a lake there, all right. It's very big, and salty."

"Could you see the other side of it? Could you tell how big it was?"

"No. Andor said it had no other side. We didn't go around to see, because the black men attacked us. There are a lot of blacks there, and they attacked us and drove us away."

"Blacks?" Talgar sounded incredulous. "But Andor said he saw no blacks at all. How is this, Andor?"

"Baltan is right," Andor answered, with impatience that he could not quite hide. "They must have arrived soon after Kelan and I left there. But it doesn't matter—the water is the most important thing."

"Blacks do matter. We must know where they come from, how many there are, all about them. You did well to find them, Baltan. But let us settle the question of the lake first. Tell us Baltan, does the lake lie on top of a mountain, as Andor said?"

Talgar silenced Andor's protest with a gesture, while Baltan struggled with the idea. "No," said Baltan, at last. "It lies between its banks, in its bed, like any lake. It couldn't stay on top of a mountain, could it? Water can't do that—it runs down."

The circle of silent men broke into a murmur, and heads nodded sagely or looked questioningly at Andor. Despite Talgar's remonstrance, Andor turned to Baltan.

"Isn't it true, Baltan, that we climbed up a long and steep pass between the two rocks, before we came to the water?"

"Yes, that's true."

"And when we came over the pass, the water on the other side was nearly as high as the pass?"

"Yes, I think so. You showed me how the water would run up over the pass and down the other side."

"If the dam—the dam that makes the high pass beyond the rocks—were to break, wouldn't the water pour down on this side?"

"Yes, you said it would."

"Don't you know it, yourself? Couldn't you see what will happen when the dam breaks?"

"But you didn't show me a dam, Andor," objected Baltan, thrown on the defensive by this catechism. "All we saw were two big rocks, like mountains, and a pass between, and a lake beyond the pass. Why didn't you show me the dam, too?"

For a moment Andor's heart stopped with the foreknowledge of defeat. For a moment only, and again he returned to the questions, though Talgar had raised a hand to interrupt.

"The pass itself is the dam. The rocks of the pass will break, and let the water into our valley. Already there are cracks and holes in it, and the water is beginning to seep through. Don't you remember the salt springs, on this side of the pass?"

**132**

"That's true," said Baltan. "There were salt springs, where we couldn't camp, and where the game wouldn't drink."

"Tell them, then, what will happen when the pass breaks, when the dam gives way or is undermined."

"You said," Baltan replied, stubbornly, "that the water would run up over the pass and down the other side."

Talgar finally succeeded in breaking in. "Can you explain to us, Baltan, how the water can run up over the pass?"

"Well, when there is a storm, Andor said that the waves splash high up on the shore. Perhaps they would splash high enough to run over on this side, but I never did understand how the whole lake could run up the slope. You remember how high the slope is, Andor. It's as long as from here to that house, at least."

"So you don't believe Andor's story. Is that what you mean?" It was Stor's voice, and Andor's temper rose at the words. But, collecting himself in time, he tried one more plea.

"Talgar—Konor—old men. Listen to me. You have sent a man to test my story—not my reasoning. He has tested it, and found it true. He is a good man, a great hunter, and a strong traveler. But he cannot see with anything but his eyes—he cannot read the secrets of the land as I can, and as you can. Can't you understand that what he is saying means that I spoke truth? The lake is there. It lies above a high pass leading down to this valley. It is already leaking through that dam —that pass. In time it will break through. When it comes, all this valley will be covered with water. What has become of the valley beyond that pass? What of the tribes who dwelt there before the water covered it? If there were any people there they perished in that flood. So shall we all if we do not move now to the mountains.

"Perhaps the flood may not come this year—perhaps not next. But some day it will come. If we have delayed moving until it comes, think of the cost of that delay! Think of your wives and children, if not of yourselves. You saw how Meltar was drowned in the river-flood, when I was a boy. So will they all drown, they and you, struggling and screaming, and there will be no shore to swim to—no shore nearer than those western peaks that you see there. Go—go to those mountains and build your houses there, before it is too late!"

He stood before them, one arm tautly outstretched toward the mountains, the other curved toward them—begging, urging, praying. The fire played tricks with the lighting on his face, so that his eyes gleamed from shadowed sockets, and the frame of disheveled hair and beard grew redly luminous against the night. His wasted body was tense with eloquence, and his voice and gestures held every listener. Then Stor stood up beside him.

The contrast was startling. Though Andor, standing alone, had looked tall because of his emaciation, he was now dwarfed by the gigantic height of Stor, whose nipples were on a level with Andor's eyes. In place of Andor's narrow and bony chest, Stor's pectoral muscles stood out in wide, thick fans, fringed with black jungle. When Stor flung out an arm like an oak limb the vision of Andor's thin pleading hands was lost. When Stor's voice issued from a cavernous beard, Andor's eloquence vanished in the booming accents of the people, saying what the people liked to hear.

**134**

"Andor," he said, "I think it is time that you stopped wasting your strength and that of the good hunters in this silly quest. Baltan went with you, and all that he says about your story is 'Andor told me this' and 'Andor told me that.' If there were this peril, couldn't Baltan have seen it for himself? There is a lake there. Well and good. There is another near the Fire Mountains. There is another below the sand hills, north of us. There are many in the forest hills beyond the Red Cliffs. But do we for that reason run to a mountain top and stay there, afraid to hunt or camp below the highest peak lest we wet our feet? Are we timid gazelles, to fly from a bird's shadow— or the shadow of one man's fear? I built a house here, and so did you—and you—and you. Will you run from them to a snowdrift in the forest, or a damp and windy cave, because Andor has had a bad dream?"

There was no mistaking the answer. Eyes blinded by tears, back bowed in defeat, Andor groped from the circle, and did not wait to hear the argument over Baltan's discovery of the blacks.

Andor hardly left his house, and spoke to no one but Bardis. He failed to note, therefore, the furtive talk among the men, the averted eyes as he passed, the smiles behind his back. But Bardis saw them, and each smile at Andor was a stab at her heart. When she thought of her babies, and how they must some day understand those smiles, it seemed unendurable.

When Stor flung out an arm like an oak limb the vision of
Andor's thin pleading hands was lost.

136

137

On the third day she walked with Andor through the olive grove that fringed the forested glade above the river. The babies, for once, she left in the care of a neighbor, but she carried a deerskin bag with which to gather olives. As she worked and he desultorily hindered her in trying to help, he opened the subject that was foremost in each mind.

"They won't go, Bardis. They won't believe me."

"I know," she replied, and paused in her picking. "I heard all the talk. I thought you spoke well and sensibly, but anybody can see that Baltan is a fool. I don't know why they listen to him."

"Nor I," said Andor. "Perhaps—perhaps that is why they sent him. No, that couldn't be. I think Talgar is ready to believe me. I think he would have understood, if I could only show him the place."

"I think any of them would, if they could see it—any but that Baltan."

"But to stay here—stay here when they must know that they will be drowned! I can't understand it. They won't face a disagreeable fact. They'd rather turn their backs on it until it comes, and tell each other it's all imagination. How can they be so blind, so lazy? Why won't they see?"

"Some day they will, Andor. Some day they will all understand, as Kelan did, and as I do now. I don't know when or how, but they will. You must never stop trying until they do, no matter what they say."

"But if it's too late?"

"That we can't help. If you stop trying to persuade them,

they'll surely be caught. If you do persuade them, they may escape. You must never stop trying."

They fell silent, and walked slowly between the olive trees, picking the fruit that the birds had spared. At length—

"Bardis," said Andor, in a new tone.

"Yes—what is it?" she answered, startled by his voice and eyes.

"Bardis, let *us* go—just you and I and the children. Let us escape this flood, and if the others won't come, they can stay. Why should we be drowned just because they're stubborn and blind?"

"But—Andor—you can't say that!"

"Why not? I've done my best. I've traveled out to the great water twice. I've fought for the idea. I've talked to them all —begged them all to save themselves. Why now should I— should you—be caught in this flood because they won't listen to me? Our babies, Bardis. Why should they . . ."

The thought was completely new to Bardis. To go—alone— just they two and the babies—into the forest—forever? No, he couldn't mean that! Andor, she thought, what are you saying? You would kill them—kill your baby daughter, away from women's help, and soft foods, and warmth. You would kill me, too. I couldn't live up there—not alone. And the boy—little Mendi. I know you'll say he'll be a man and a hunter, but he's not yet. This is only his third summer—no, his fourth. He's a baby. You can't mean it.

Though these thoughts crowded her mind, she kept silence for a time. When she spoke only the extreme softness of her voice betrayed her excitement—her terror.

**139**

"No, we can't, Andor. We can't go away and leave them all. How would we feel, if we alone were left? How could we live alone in the forest, in the cold mountains?"

"But, dear Bardis, we can't live down here. If we stay here we shall die—you and I, and the babies as well. The forest may not be so nice as this is now, but we can live there. We have before, you know—you and I."

"That was different—that was just a hunting trip, but we couldn't do even that, with the children."

Again a long silence, less peaceful than the last—a little more constrained. Andor ceased his intermittent olive picking, and stared over the bright plain to the southwest, brown and yellow now with the autumn drought. That's where it's coming from, he told himself. Always watch there.

Then he returned to the subject. "If we know the flood is coming, and we know we can't get anyone else to go away, then we must take the children and go alone, mustn't we?"

"No—no!" said Bardis. "Our friends—my father and mother —how can we go away from them? How can we leave all these people, this safe home, to wander in the snow because of an imaginary flood?"

A word stopped Andor's inattentive mind. "Imaginary?" he asked. "Did you say imaginary?"

"Well, it—it isn't here, is it?" Bardis's pale smile appeared and faded. "That makes it imaginary, doesn't it? At least, in a way."

"Bardis," said Andor, solemnly, and took her by both shoulders. "Do you believe me?"

"Of course, Andor."

**140**

"How much?"

"Why, in everything."

"Enough to come with me to the mountains, if I say so?"

Was this the final word? Would her answer decide their relationship forever? Oh, she couldn't let it come to that—not yet! Andor was sick and weak. He didn't know what he was saying, what he was asking of her. She mustn't be asked to decide—later, later, but not yet. Desperately she looked away from his face. Desperately her mind sought for a pinhole of escape from the question. Time passed.

"Answer me, Bardis," said Andor, very gently.

Wildly she stared into his eyes. Oh, he couldn't ask that of her—he couldn't. He was just home. He wasn't well. He didn't know . . .

"Yes, Andor, yes," she gasped, and as her tears came he lowered her gently to the ground. "Oh, Andor—our home, our friends, our life. What shall we do? How can we go? What if the babies are sick? Oh, Andor, what if I have another baby? Oh, what shall we do? Andor, you won't—you couldn't!"

Andor laid his hand on her hot forehead, and she seized it in both of hers. Gently he withdrew it, and walking a few steps, stopped and stared again at the endless plain. There. Always watch there.

Bardis, save for her racking sobs, was silent. He came back and knelt beside her. Then he kissed her wet cheeks and hair.

"We won't go, Bardis," he said.

The earth turned on her unhurried course, and the seasons brought storm and peace, plenty and poverty, life and death, to her myriad children. Silently, confidently, the architecture of the world took shape. Northward moved the ice that had hidden half of Europe at its height, and northward moved the forests to preempt the land it left. The melting of the great glaciers swelled the seas of the world, and the waters crept imperceptibly up their measureless shores, the rising lost in the constant fluctuation of wave and tide.

Other changes, too, went forward, and, step by slow step, Europe's face changed toward the face it was to present to Caesar's exploring legions. As the sea rose it encroached upon the flat plains that lay between Britain and Germany, so that when the ice finally withdrew, the plains were washed by the shallow North Sea. To the south of the great valley the uplands grew drier and hotter, forming more and more a barrier to man between the steaming tropics and the cool forests of Europe.

But one great step remained. No sea separated Europe and Africa. Only the placid reaches of the great valley had to be crossed, in order to walk from Europe's wilderness to Africa's deserts. The ocean that would wreak that change, that would bear this child among oceans, still stood patiently behind Gibraltar's barrier, awaiting her deliverance.

These alterations of climate, and of land and sea, progressed with infinite slowness, so that to a man observing the world about him they were not apparent. Just so the butterfly, flitting a few brief days through the dappled shade of

**142**

oak leaves, sees in the oak an eternal, unvarying structure. It cannot even see the gradual process by which the mantle of leaves hides the branches, or falls and reveals their starkness when summer is done. The squirrel can see this annual change, but even to it the growth of the oak from seedling to forest patriarch is unrevealed and inconceivable.

To the tribe, living through years of hardship and of ease, suffering, working, dying, but always gaining a little on balance from the hard world they fought, the changes in the face of the earth were as slow, as foreign, as unthought of, as would the growth of the oak be to the butterfly in its shade. Even if Konor, or old Iri, who became the dean of the tribe on Konor's death, said the winters were warmer than he remembered as a boy, there was always another on hand to recall some incident to prove the reverse. It was never even an interesting subject for idle talk. Too many immediate problems faced them, and engrossed in these, the tribesmen knew or cared nothing of the great and silent history being written on the hills and valleys of the earth.

To Andor alone had there been vouchsafed a glimpse of one of the steps in the process. But as the years passed, and the flood he prophesied still withheld its hand, his tale, discredited from the first, became almost forgotten, save that the phrase "Andor's flood" survived as a derisive byword. He and Bardis stayed on and on in the village, while Mendi grew to man's stature and age, and little Andis turned from a round soft bundle to a flutter of thin arms and legs, and suddenly, to a lovely woman.

But, though Bardis's woman's tasks kept her close to, and

**143**

on good terms with, the other women of the tribe, Andor, though with the village, was not of it. His voice was no longer raised at the council fire, for it had too long been received with smiling disregard. He hunted, it is true, for the common larder as well as his own, but he hunted always alone. More and more frequently he would disappear for weeks and months together, on his endless trips of exploration. Sometimes Mendi went with him, but Mendi now was married to Talsa's daughter, Talsa of the Black Hammer, whose strength and sense had made him chief over the less popular Stor. Then, too, Mendi had so many interests of his own that it seemed hard for him to pay to Andor's problems, the undivided attention that his father seemed to demand.

So Andor was alone again. Alone he walked from Gibraltar to the Ice Mountains themselves, trying to carry a level in his eye—trying to see what part of the ragged country between would be above the coming sea. Alone he explored the peaks of Corsica and the great plateau of Sardinia. Alone he penetrated the fearful chasm by the Fire Mountains where, dim in a future that now is dim in the past, would roar the paired rock and whirlpool of Ulysses. Alone he searched the bitter valleys of the Pyrenees, aloof and hostile to this child of their own strayed children. All the time he sought—sometimes dully and mechanically, sometimes with unreasoning optimism, for a place to which he could persuade the tribe to move and be safe.

All the while, beyond the western rocks, the sea ground at the shore, hammering, probing, testing for the flaw that would spell its release. Every year a minute portion of

**144**

strength was added to it, as the melting glaciers gave back to it the waters they had sequestered. Every year its time grew nearer. As if arraying itself for the coming immolation, the valley seemed to bloom more luxuriantly each spring, and to furnish more riches of game and fruit each autumn, so that with happiness and plenty, the little heedless world within it moved toward its ending.

It was on Andor's return from one of his trips of exploration that Bardis met him with the news that Andis was to be married to young Milor.

Andor was pleased, but absently so. He had seen little of Andis these past years, and understood as little. She, on her part, loved him warmheartedly, but quite uncomprehendingly, and blushed with pleasure when her playmates told her that they liked her despite her funny father.

It was different with Mendi. As a boy he was in fight after fight, defending his father from the unthinking adolescent laughter that he heard. Because of his muscular prowess the boys were soon careful to control their laughter in his presence, but even as a married man he still fought occasionally. Deadlier encounters, these, that had cost Mendi an eye and left him a host of scars. The process had made him somber and almost surly, both with outsiders and with his parents. Only his little plump wife seemed to know how to conquer his moods.

Once his daughter was married, Andor sought out Bardis, and laid before her an idea that had grown in his mind. "Up in the Ice Mountains," he began, "I have found a cave. When I found it I was trailing a deer, and being hungry I couldn't stop to look at it closely. But it was easy to see that people had lived there once. Outside the cave the cliff-wall was black with old fires. Broken flints lay here and there. A well-worn path led into it, but that may be kept open by animals.

"Now this place, though low down in the Ice Mountains themselves, is high enough to be out of the flood, I am sure. I think it might be an ideal place for the people to live while they are building the new village in the mountains. There is plenty of game and water, and it's not so high up that the winters would be too severe to be borne.

"Our children are both married, and yet we are young and strong. Let's go and live in the cave, just for the rest of this summer. There's nothing more for us to do here, at least until the larder-stocking in the fall. Our hunting and our work wouldn't be missed. When we come back we'll be able to show them how they can live up there, better even than here. Perhaps, at long last, they will move."

Bardis's objections were feeble—not because of lack of work at home, but because of her remembrance of the promise she had made to Andor, many years ago, in answer to his question, "Enough to come with me to the mountains if I say so?" He had not exacted that sacrifice then, nor had he ever presumed on the promise until now, in this small way. Rather, he had sacrificed himself to years of daily terror for

**146**

her and her children's safety. She could guess at his state of mind on his long trips, when he must have climbed every hill that gave an outlook over the valley, and searched the distance for the glimmer of the flood. Could she now deny him this simple request?

But when he said they were both young and strong although their children were married, she knew he was wrong. He could not see himself—wiry and slight, it is true, but bent with the years, and gray on brow and chin. Her own hair was still black, which made it harder for Andor to see within her, and know how it was with her. In all those months of his long absences, there had been nothing for her but work, and work she did, as long as her strength allowed —for her children first, for others next, for herself last. But the work had taken its toll, and she knew, without the skill of physicians, that her worn body had almost run its course. There was no self-reproach in the knowledge, nor complaining that the sands had run too fast. It did not occur to her that she could postpone the end by shirking the tasks of the house, or, if it did, she knew it was untrue. So many years of work, so many winters of hunger, so many summers of labor, and the life-spring was exhausted.

Yet she did not fear death. She never questioned her reunion with Andor in the land of the dead beyond the Pyrenees. And she longed with a mute longing for the restful stillness of that sleep. It should not be long, now, in coming.

"Of course I'll go, Andor," she said.

"We'll start in two days, then," he replied. "You'd better get a little dried meat, to save hunting, and some warm skins.

**147**

It's a little colder up there than down here," he added, apologetically.

Bardis paused by her house—the same house that Andor had built for her in the flush of their youth and love—many, many warm years ago. In one sense it was not the same house, for, piece by fallen piece, it had been replaced time and again. The roof beams were still there, and the flat stones that underlay the clay walls. But again and again had Andor pulled down a crumbling section of wall, and replaced it with new tiers of mud bricks. Almost every year the thatch had been renewed. Even the hide over the door had never lasted more than a few years of the children's tuggings. But nonetheless, it was the same house that had risen, solid and safe and comforting, under Andor's laboring hands.

Bardis stopped in its shade, and traced with strong, tired fingers the seams and fissures in the wall. Here, close by the door, the print of Andor's hand was preserved, in false immortality, in the rough patching of clay that he had pressed into place. The fingers of children, sliding unheedingly over the walls in their play, had already dulled the outlines of that imprint. Here was another crack, that had afforded shelter to some wandering grass-seed. From it there now sprouted a tiny green forest, through which an undaunted ant struggled to some indistinct but urgent goal. To the ant the forest was part of the immutable world, his engrossing task mercifully keeping from him the chance of reflecting and observing the change that abides in all things. To the grass, content to exist wherever nourishment could

**148**

be coaxed, its only questing the vicarious one of sending its errant seeds free upon the wind, the wall was part of the changeless earth, and as immortal. But to Bardis, as her fingers idly brushed the grass and the sun-warmed clay, nothing any more seemed eternal.

Her house was fragile, and must be patched and shored to meet each recurrent storm. Her children had changed from warm helpless babies to inquiring awkward youngsters, and now to self-reliant grown people. Even the broad earth whereon the village stood had always seemed impermanent, uncertain, since Andor had told her that it must one day die under the sea. Andor himself—he around whom her life had been woven as the silk about the chrysalis, the vine about the tree—even Andor was changing with the years.

It was hard for her to remember much about her little life before she became his. Andor, from the day he first spoke to her, here on the river's bank, had been her captain, steering her where he would.

She smiled palely as she thought of that. True, his had been the rushing force of thought that impelled his mind to discoveries, and his body to prowess. But without her, how would he have nursed his strength through those gray days of reaction and discouragement that followed? She knew her own part in his life, and knew it had been worthy.

Together they started for the mountains, carrying weapons and a little food. It surprised and pained Andor to find how slow their progress was. He, who alone had crisscrossed the great valley with his tracks, who could outlast most of the younger men on the trail, now had to cramp his step and cut his marches to a pattern that his wife could follow. But his patience and consideration kept these feelings from her, and at last they found themselves breasting the daunting slopes that ended in the Pyrenean ice. The forests bubbled with bird-song under the probing fingers of the young sun. Violets and cyclamen nodded to their feet, and tendrils of eglantine snatched at their legs, as if to keep them out of these hallowed hills. Andor's eyes slid constantly from sunlit branch to shadowed hollow, noting automatically each movement of a leaf, and ascribing to it its cause—the jiggle of an alighting bird, the soft retreat of some watching animal, or merely the wanderings of the wind.

The day was still soft and young when they reached the gently sloping shelf they had been seeking. From it the land fell, step by step, through the forests of France. Behind it the tall spruces pointed the way to the peaks, still wrapped in their icy mantle. In the clear light, distances became dwarfed, and their long climb up the slope looked in retrospect like a few minutes' walk. They squatted here to rest, while the grandeur of the vista held them silent.

Then they crossed the rolling surface of the shelf, threading their way through brambles and hardwood thickets, to the foot of the next step upward in the path to the peaks and passes above. The step here was nearly sheer, a lime-

**150**

stone cliff hung with vine clusters and glistening with seep-
age. In its cool surface was hollowed out the mouth of the
cavern they had been seeking.

The tunnel led into darkness that their sun-squinted eyes
could not penetrate. Its mouth was half hidden in luxuriant
growth, through which a rivulet gleamed. Beside the stream
ran a narrow, well-worn path. Peering carefully through the
parted leaves, Andor saw the antechamber, cool and dimly
lit. On its ceiling played dancing lights, thrown up by the
little stream as it rippled into the sunlight. On its floor were
random piles of sticks and bones. A scent of fox was in the
air, and another smell, fainter but indefinably hostile.

"Be careful, Andor," whispered Bardis. "There may be
wolves in there."

"Not in this moon," he answered. "They only live here in
cubbing time, in the spring. There might be a fox or two but
no wolves."

They backed out into the sunlight, and sat to consider
their next course. Andor glanced sharply at Bardis a moment,
for he noticed how wearily she slumped to the ground as
they rested, one handed pressed momentarily against her
heart, but her next remark drove the thought from his mind.
As her eyes traced the cliff that cut into the sky behind them,
she suddenly pointed.

"See that cliff, Andor—see how it looks just like a man's
face! There is the eye, and there the mouth, and that cluster
of trees below makes a beard."

Andor stared along her pointed finger, and his voice, when
he spoke, had dropped with awe.

*151*

"Do you remember the words of the song—

'The cave that was painted
With years and with days.
The cave that the north wind
Never could find.
The cave that the Old Man
Watched with one eye.'?

"There is the Old Man, and here, behind us, is the cave—our people's cave."

They fell silent, their eyes moving between the cave mouth in the shadow of the spruces and that gigantic profile cut against the sky. Through the ranks of the pillared forest, fallen silent while the birds rested through the noon, Andor stared dreamily, and long thoughts took his mind back to the songs of his people's history. He could almost see the tall hunters bringing meat through the forest, while in the patches of sunlight, now tangled in rich, leafy neglect, he imagined the women, squatting to their work, gossiping over the whispered rasp of the hide-scrapers. Here must have dwelt Osor the Finder, and through this shadowy sunlight the great Hastor must have walked, a dreaming boy. But now, over their strong, happy voices, lay the silence of desertion.

From this cave, from the watchful eye of that stone face on the cliff, his tribe—his own forefathers, and Bardis's—his boyhood idols of strength and wisdom—had gone forth, to settle in the great valley below, and build their homes and rear their babies by the white river of the south. To the eyes

*152*

of that time, in the knowledge of that day, it had seemed a move of great wisdom and foresight. It had brought them happiness and a measure of ease, so that venturesome men found time to invent and explore, and venturesome minds had strength to wonder. It had given the makers of songs, Tanda and Eral, and fat Pilor the Nightingale, time to sit idle in the evenings, and compose the long chants enshrining the deeds of the men of old.

But what a fatal mistake it was proving! Andor alone knew what the outcome of it must be. He alone saw clearly the end of the blind trail on which they had embarked.

It was within his power to see this, clearly and tragically, but it was beyond his strength—tantalizingly beyond it—to avert the disaster. He had learned nothing new about his problem by finding the cave, but he felt that it had revivified the issue in his flagging mind. To see the very stones the feet of his ancestors had worn smooth, to breathe the clear wind of the heights, was to see the more sharply the error of their move to the valley, and the urgency, and the impossibility, of retracing that step. Like the ocean that he had found, he must spend the years hammering at the stone wall resisting him. But unlike the ocean, which would one day carry the ramparts by its ceaseless assault, his efforts must inevitably decrease with age and exhaustion, and the wall would only grow stronger and stronger under his attacks.

Bardis interrupted his thoughts. "I feel tired, Andor," she said, "and I don't think I can hunt today, but we must have some meat before we can make a camp here. Will you hunt, while I rest? Then, if you have luck, we can sleep here, and tomorrow we can explore the cave."

Dreamily Andor did as she suggested. Even in his distraction he hunted silently and keenly. His reward was a yearling reindeer, an unfamiliar animal to the plains-dwellers, but a very welcome beginning for the larder. While the sun was still high he carried it back to where Bardis lay resting in a shady thicket, and together they skinned it, and ate of the tender meat.

The meal done and the hide hung to dry, they sat in the open to watch the sun withdraw from the great ranges and plains before them. Around them, under the branches, night's dusky fingers were laying the first shadows. The birds grew silent, and the wind paused as if to do homage to the aging day.

The dazzling ice-fields caught the light of the sunset, and its warm glow seemed to mitigate for a time their eternal cold. The ranks of tall spruces, marching with infinite persistence up the slopes, grew dark and hazy.

"This will do," said Andor, softly. "This is where the village should be built. See the clay, here, for making bricks. See how this little stream, running out of the cave, would flow right through the center of the village, so that there would be no need to carry water. The people could live in the cave until the houses are finished, just as they lived so many years ago. There is an abundance of game, even when

**154**

the snow lies deep in winter. Above all, the flood can never reach here."

Bardis answered nothing, but twisted her fingers in her lap. The rosy light faded from the peaks, that now stood hard and bitter against the dove-gray sky. After a space Andor noticed his wife's silence.

"Don't you think it might do?" he asked.

"Yes," she answered, abstractedly.

"But you are thinking something else, too," persisted Andor. "I know what it is. You are thinking that I should give up this quest, and live quietly like the others in the village so that people wouldn't laugh at me as they now do. Aren't you?"

"Oh, yes, yes, Andor!" Bardis's eyes dimmed and her throat tightened as the words tumbled forth. "Oh, Andor, if you only would! If you only knew what it has been to me to see scorn in people's faces—scorn for my husband. Why do you go on, Andor? You know that the tribe will never move here—will never move anywhere. You know that we cannot move without them, that I couldn't live here, alone with you in the forest. Why don't you give it up? You have done all that you can do—no one else could have done half as much. Give it up, my husband, and live with me in peace among our people. We are old people, now, old and tired, and we should rest, rest and live quietly among our friends."

"And the flood?" asked Andor, slowly. "Don't you believe that it's coming?"

"Of course I do—you must know that. But it may not come until after we are dead, so that it won't matter to us.

Wouldn't it be better to forget it, to be respected again in the tribe, to live as others do?"

"For one who could do it," he replied, "it might be better, and easier, to forget the flood. I could not. I know the suffering it has caused you, and I have wept for you, when I was alone in the hills, but it could not have been otherwise, and it cannot be now."

"Haven't you given up hope? Isn't it clear that no one will ever listen to you?"

"Not quite. No one has listened yet—no one but my own family, and Kelan, but some day he may come, the boy with the vision to believe an old man's tale, and the ability to make the people understand. Alone I can never do it. I know that now. But if I can ever find him, then it can be done. You see, therefore, why I must not stop?"

The peaks grew darker, and far to the east a spot on the horizon brightened with the coming moon. The two were silent, watching the golden disk, that moved into the sky with the deliberation of eternity. For a space it was clouded and darkened by the vapors of the earth, and then it climbed free, to shine at last with the unattainable purity of the heavens.

As it rose it spread its quiet radiance over the vastness of the valley, and picked out, with jagged lines of black and gray and silver, the ice-crowned range before them. The silence was heightened, not broken, by the distant wolf-call, and by the movements of tiny night-creatures around them. Andor's voice, when he spoke again, might have come from an embodiment of the night—from the moon, who saw the

**156**

whole valley and knew its days were numbered—from the distant, patient sea, confident of conquest.

"Whether the people ever believe it or not, whether they escape it or not, still the flood will come."

From across the eastern horizon, from the slopes of the long Appenines, where dwelt as yet only the beasts and birds of the silent forest, came the foreknowledge of a whisper that was to repeat Andor's words in the unconceived future; a whisper that was to ring louder than the shouts of conquering armies or the brazen trumpets of kings. Borne on an east wind out of the highlands, it passed almost audibly through the air about them. "E pur si muove," it said. "But still it moves."

As if to echo those unthought words of Galileo, his primitive precursor sighed and repeated his last sentence. "Still the flood will come," he said.

"But if it does, Andor, and the people are all caught in it, of what use is all this searching and exploring for new village-sites?"

"When it comes, I do not know how fast the waters will rise. It may be that they will come slowly enough to let us escape. If that happens, we must know of a place to go, and of the quickest path to reach it. Therefore I continue to search."

Bardis did not reply, but sat with her hand pressed to her breast, while Andor watched the moon moving among the bashful stars. At last they slept, while above them, patient as the stars, outliving the trees, aging only as the mountains aged, the profile of the Old Man gazed unsleeping into the night, awaiting the return of his people.

With the morning light they explored the cave. Beyond the narrow entrance was a wide chamber, its floor dry and sandy, and heaped with bones. The curious smell they had first noticed faintly haunted the air. Along the floor they built little fires, which led them, step by step, into the farther windings of the cave. With a boy's delight, Andor gathered fragments left by the people of the old time—flint knives and spears, chipped to the precise and delicate outline of willow leaves—hide scrapers, heavier, and with one straight blade—and stone axes girdled with a groove to receive the split handle.

There were seashells, which seemed to have been used as vessels, but all were broken. Perhaps they had been brought, in the cloudy past, from the same sea that Andor had found, but their discoverer had glimpsed nothing of Andor's vision, and his trip had not even been preserved in a song. Andor felt a moment's surge of sympathy for that ancient explorer, who had stood on the threshold of a great and crushing discovery, and who had died without realizing it.

It was Bardis who discovered the paintings on the walls, and, discovering them, gained a childish excitement over the exploration. Between them they traced, by the dancing light of their fires, the crude but magnificent murals. Here and

**158**

there they were obliterated by new mud, and the pigment had been rubbed off in some spots, perhaps by animals, but in the dim and smoky light, they seemed to draw a curious life from their flickering illumination.

"What are these little lines, Andor," cried Bardis, "row after row of them, and little pictures of animals above them?"

Again the words of the old song came to Andor's mind. " 'The cave that was painted with years and with days,' " he quoted. "That's it! The animals are the names of the years. That's why the song says:

> 'In the year of the bison
> Osor went forth.'

That's it—that must be it.

> 'Osor went forth
> And saw the white river
> That drew all the game.' "

"Osor persuaded the tribe to move down to the valley, didn't he?" Bardis's voice was timid.

"So the song says." Suddenly their elation died in thoughtfulness. As their voices ceased, the jealous silence of the cave rushed in to its accustomed sway, and lay upon them, tangible, oppressive. The dead past stood at their shoulders, and stole the lightness from their hearts.

Where there had been movement and voices and laughter, there was now this stillness. Where warm bodies had lain in slumber or moved in life, there was only the damp rock, guarding in the darkness the broken fragments that the

**159**

people had deserted. Andor broke the stillness in a hushed tone.

"Osor persuaded them to go down to the river from here," he said. "He saw that game was thicker, and that the snow did not burden the ground as it does here. But it meant to the tribe that they must sacrifice their safe, warm cave for the night of desolation on the plains, until Hastor showed them how to build new little caves of their own. It meant hardship, uncertainties, and change. Above all, change. I wonder how he persuaded them to do it."

Again the silence, while the fires burned dimly in the death-like air. Bardis, remembering the cool feel of the wind of the plains, when it caressed a tired body, could see one of the disadvantages of the cave, as well.

"Perhaps the hunting wasn't good here," continued Andor, monotonously. "Perhaps they were hungry, and were willing to follow anyone who could show them more food. That may have been why it was easier for Osor to persuade them than for me.

"Or the tribe may have been much smaller, so that the word of one man counted for more. Moreover, the winters must have been long and cold up here. It may have been in the autumn that they went down, fearing the cold.

"Osor was a great hunter, stronger than anyone in the tribe. The song says:

> 'His spear was a tree
> Pointed with onyx,
> His hammer a cliff
> That fell upon wolves.

**160**

His eyes were a wind
That frightened the birds,
His feet pressed the grass
Where the horses had fled.'

It would be easy for such a one to rule the tribe with his word—easier than for me."

Bardis, her heart sore for the pain in her husband's voice, could say nothing. Andor continued.

"It was a change, but a change from hardship to ease, from hunger to plenty, from cold to warmth. Our change must be otherwise. Osor could still tell them that their cave would always be here, if the new life proved less desirable than they hoped. I must tell them that they must never return, no matter what trials the new home holds in store. Mine is the harder task."

"Yes—harder," whispered Bardis.

"Our people have grown used to small, clean houses," continued Andor, "and we must bring them to a single damp cave. They have grown up with the wind of the plains in their nostrils, and we must close them in a forest and a cavern. They have become accustomed to a gentle winter, with a few weeks of rain, and we can only offer them months of snow and hunger. It will be hard."

"Yes—too hard," said Bardis.

Andor shook himself out of his reverie. "I want to go farther back in the cave before we go out," he said. "Meanwhile, you might bring the deer-hide in, so that we can scrape it and cure it with bark."

*Then he turned a corner, and met the origin of the smell.*

**162**

He picked up a burning stick as a torch, and penetrated the blackness beyond the last of their fires. As he advanced, the unfamiliar smell which he had first noticed when he entered the cave grew stronger, and with it a faint stench of carrion. Then he turned a corner, and met the origin of the smell.

It was a bear—but no such bear as he had ever seen before. Its vast shoulders towered higher than his own head, and its head and jaws, swinging restlessly from side to side, were in themselves as big as half an ordinary bear. It emitted a rumble from its throat that echoed fearsomely down the black corridor. Bardis heard it, and her heart froze in terror.

"What is it, Andor? What is it?" she called.

Andor waved his burning stick to brighten the flames. "A bear," he answered, "a giant bear! Run outside of the cave and hide. I can keep him off with the fire!"

The bear, still rocking absurdly back and forth, began advancing slowly. Andor backed step by step away, holding his stick as near as he dared to the flaming little eyes, almost hidden in their furry sockets. Behind him he heard a gasping scream from Bardis, and knew she was outside the cave. "Are you hidden?" he called. The bear rumbled another growl, which drowned her answer.

Clearly Andor could not hold the beast off much longer, especially as his burning stick threatened to go out momentarily. He decided to risk a dash. With one motion he tossed his brand into the bear's eyes, and with the next he wheeled and plunged through the cave's door. At the entrance he turned sharply, and swung himself part way up the cliff on the tangled vines.

The roar from the cave, muffled though it was, was terrifying. Blinded by the sparks, its fur smouldering, the great beast charged out of the mouth of the cavern. Without pausing to look around, it crashed off into the forest, dazzled as much by the sudden light as by the burning stick. Andor could hear the sounds of its mad flight grow fainter and finally cease.

Elated, he called to Bardis. To his surprise there was no reply. He called again, and again. Then he began a search that became more frantic as it continued.

At length he found her. She was lying on her face, in a thicket a few paces from the cave, and to his horror she did not respond to his voice. He knelt quickly beside her, and turned her face up to his. Then, slowly and heavily, her eyelids opened, and after a moment she whispered his name.

"Andor," she said, "are you safe? Is it gone?"

"Of course I am," he smiled. "The bear ran away, with his fur on fire. We're quite safe. He won't come back."

Her eyes closed again in utter weariness, and a cold fear invaded Andor's stomach.

"What's the matter, Bardis? What is it? What's wrong? Say something. We're all safe. The bear's gone."

Bardis did not answer, but lay, a dead weight, on his arm. Slowly her right hand stole to her heart, as if to reply by a sign to his question. Then her eyes opened again.

"Andor," she whispered feebly, "something has happened to me, here. I'm going to die. I would rather die, anyway,

**165**

here, alone with you in the forest. Do you remember how we went into the forest together, first? Do you remember how you said, when we were both children, that you would find the cave, and I asked you to take me with you? You did, didn't you? So now we've done it, and I can go."

Her eyes closed again, and suddenly the life went out of her face as the sun vanishes behind a winter cloud. The smooth forehead, the faintly wrinkled eyelids, the patient tired mouth, all were unchanged, but Bardis was gone, and would not return. As Andor moved his support, her hand slipped from her heart to her side, and he saw again the sunken breasts that had nourished his children, and the frail slim body that had borne them. The sight brought him full and overwhelming realization, and he bowed his head above her in despair.

When he had buried Bardis, beside the little stream that flowed from the cave mouth, and had laid beside her body some of the reindeer meat, wrapped carefully in a piece of the hide, Andor knew he should go home. The work, done with numb mind and blind eyes, had served to keep him from thinking. Now there was nothing more to be done, except to go home. Home? When Bardis would not be there to meet him? When home meant the bachelors' house, where perhaps they would give him a corner to sit in, and a bone to gnaw? Home? And yet he must go.

He looked down at the crude grave, piled with the largest

stones he could carry. Just so had he buried Kelan, on that far-off hill by the western river. What had he done? How had this vision of his, this curse of his so blighted and killed the only two friends that had understood it? The only two friends he had ever had. It had killed them both, and still spared him.

Was it Andor, not the vision, who had killed them? Perhaps it was. Perhaps it had been his selfishness, his insistence on his own course. And Kelan and Bardis were its victims. But could it be selfishness? Had he gained anything, or even hoped to gain anything, by his extraordinary vision? Yes, once he had. Once he had imagined that his prophecy would bring him honor among the people, that it would end his hateful position as Andor the Little. But that had not been for long. Soon, soon it had become clear that, though he ceased being Andor the Little, it was only to become Andor the Mad.

Couldn't he have stopped then? Forgotten the flood, forgotten that terrible pass between the western rocks, and lived as other people lived? Even though he kept alive the knowledge in his mind, couldn't he have curbed his tongue, when he saw how useless his warnings became? It would have spared Bardis years of a suffering that he could only guess at. It would have spared her this lonely death.

What had he done to his children? How blighted Mendi's bright questioning eyes, and turned him into the dour man who walked friendless through the happy tribe? And Andis? Her light heart seemed to cast off every shadow that fell on it, but how much of that was real and how much defensive armor? How much had she really suffered, behind that happy mask, over the ridicule which he had brought upon himself? And to no end.

Deeper than all, that thought dug its rapier into his heart. To no end. The tribe still lived carefree in their village, the ocean still cut ceaselessly at its barrier. The flood would still come, and it would be as if Andor had never lived, or never seen his terrifying vision. Uselessly had he lived and suffered. Uselessly had these two friends died for him. Uselessly would he go on.

An old man, his spirit dead within him, his steps trembling with fatigue, Andor returned to the tribe. From the first hilltop that gave an outlook over his valley he stopped, as he always had done, and stared over the southern plains. Always watch there. But for what? Why avoid the flood now? He could not answer, could only stare with eyes that swam with sorrow.

With Mendi and his wife, and with Andis and her husband, he made another pilgrimage to Bardis's grave. It was autumn in the mountains. The aspen groves flashed golden amid the bronze-green of the oaks. The nights were diamond-clear and cold. The forest made ready, with bared branches and leaf-strewn earth, for the winter's vigil. Above the trees stared the cold profile of the Old Man, unmoved by seasons, or by life and death. The little group about the grave drew their wolf-hide garments closer about them, as the breath of the ice fields sought them out under the trees.

Nothing was said, for all knew that there was nothing that could be worth saying. But Mendi walked by his father's side down the homeward hill, and his hand did not leave Andor's shoulder.

Slowly the moon turned her silver face from the earth, and slowly brought it around in tireless sequence. Slowly the years melted into greenness, and faded with the fading sun. In the village life's cycle revolved, and soft babies grew to shrill children, and children into men and women. But of these things Andor had no part. Although he toiled and rested with the others, although he traveled and hunted and labored on the houses, it was with empty arms and heart that he lived, growing imperceptibly grayer and slower of movement with the rolling years.

Always he waited, for two events that came to seem as one to his loneliness. He waited for the flood, and for his permission to join Bardis, beyond the silver portal of the moon.

No wonder, thought Andor, as the years dragged on, no wonder that the tribe should tolerate him now. They had beaten him—Stor and the tribe. They could afford the little generosity. Stor and the tribe, and the flood, too, had beaten him—that flood that unaccountably held off from year to year. He longed to make another journey to the western rocks, to see the progress of his prophecy, but it was too obviously beyond his strength. He suggested to Mendi, on one of the few days when he succeeded in talking freely with his son, that the younger man should make the trip, but Mendi found excuses. There was nothing left to do but to watch—there, to the south, where it would first appear.

On the swelling ridge behind the village there was a group of little cedars—little and old and twisted from lifetimes of struggle against insufficient water and a lean soil. They were the last outpost of the northern forest at this point. Below them the ridge fell off to the south, so that a man might see, from a seat near the cedars, all the wide plain to east and south and west. A fallen log, at the edge of this group of trees, in time became Andor's second home. Too feeble to hunt, he would take a strip of meat from the common larder, and painfully climb the slope up which, a few years ago, he would have run without a quickened breath. Seated on the log, his headless hammer shaft across his knees, he would alternately doze and stare at the southern horizon, until his old eyes watered with the effort.

While sitting so throughout the endless, aimless days, he hummed to himself the words of a song—a song that had never been sung aloud, that would never stir the blood of the young men as the old men chanted it in winter twilights. It was a song that he had made himself, and that no ear would ever hear. Unconsciously his fist beat time on the log to the soundless measures.

> "Out of the sunset
> Out of the star home
> Out of the land
> Of the thorn and the desert,

Down from the heights
Of the rocks of the sunset
Came the great waters
That Andor had seen.
Came with a roar
And a tumult of waters,
Came with a wail
And a crying of sea-birds,
Came with the wind
And the growling of thunder,
Came with the rain
And the sound of the storm.
High in the mountains,
Safe in the mountains,
Safe in the cave
Of the Old Man's mountains
The men and the children,
The women, the old men,
Watched while the waters
Devoured the valley,
Watched while the waters
Devoured their homes.
In the cave that was painted
With years and with days,
In the cave that the Old Man
Watched with one eye,
In the cave that is marked
By the grave of Bardis,
The people are living
In joy and in plenty,
The people are living
In safety once more.
For Andor the Little
Had told of the waters,

Andor the Little
Had warned of the flood.
Now by the cave
And the gravestone of Bardis
The song of Andor
Is sung again.
Now with the eye
Of the Old Man upon us
The song of Andor
We sing again."

Almost he could hear the singing, see the people sitting in silence under the ageless trees, smell the wood smoke from that fire that would never be lighted. In his life there was little difference, now, between the dream and the reality, and often the dark cave where Bardis lay was as real to him as this sun-beaten plain.

Stor, alone of his contemporaries, also had survived the years. Stor, too, was a shrunken remnant of the magnificent animal of a generation ago. The great skeleton was there, brittle and stiff with age, but the meat was gone from collar bone and rib and shank, and the black tangle of hair and beard had faded to white strings. The arm that once had thrown a stallion in its stride now carried only a staff to aid the faltering legs.

But Stor still knew and loved the hunt. He could not join, but he could watch from the same sentinel cedar grove that sheltered Andor's vigil, while the young men drove and attacked the little herds of game that dotted the plain below. He would grunt and rumble in disgust, and rehearse each failure around the village fires at the end of the day. Occasionally his comments seemed too urgent to keep until the evening, and he would call them out to Andor, seated beneath a neighboring tree. That was not very satisfactory, however, for usually Andor had been asleep, or lost in contemplation of the blue horizon, and had not seen the point in question. For the most part, therefore, the two old men sat, only a tree or two between them, in a silence whose hostility was almost visible.

New faces ringed the council fires, and new voices sang the age old songs at twilight. Strange young women, with familiar names, labored over the endless tasks of food and clothes and shelter. Talsis, stout and cheerful and wrinkled, presided over the house of black-visaged Mendi, whose beard turned iron gray although his strength remained. Her father was dead, and his place as chief was taken by Konor, grandson of the old Konor who was dean of the tribe in Andor's youth.

Andis, his daughter, had changed little in becoming a mother and a grandmother. She was thin and wrinkled, and her once dusty brown hair was nearly all gray. But she was still the slightly irresponsible child who had worried Bardis, and had blushed for her father among her playmates. Andor felt closer to his grandchildren than to this once lovely daughter.

Old and young, differing widely from each other as always, the people differed only in nonessentials from the tribe that Andor had first known. Just as cheerfully or sorrowfully they lived out their hard lives, and moved just as blindly a step closer to their destiny.

**173**

To Andor on his cedar log came Milis, Andis's eldest daughter, and now herself the mother of three children. Though her little ones regarded old Andor with too much terror to make him their playmate, Milis, alone among her brothers and cousins, had always felt close to the old man. She it was who brought him his food, to spare him an extra descent from his lookout seat. She it was who saw that he had a good hide to wear, and who attended to his little comforts. And of all Bardis's grandchildren, Milis resembled her most closely—the same slender figure, grave, oval face, and raven hair that had twisted Andor's heart with love, long years ago.

Now she brought him meat, and stood idly by while he munched it, smiling at her his thanks. As she stood, her eyes drifted over the hot plain below, where the tiny figures of the hunters looked like ants against the yellow-green carpet of the grass. Then she stared more fixedly.

Never had the sunlight glistened so on the southern plains. It was almost as if they were covered with water—as if a great lake had appeared there. Water! To her mind rushed the all-but-forgotten story. It was Andor's flood!

She seized the old man's arm. "Andor—Andor—look!" she cried. "Your flood! It's here—it's coming!"

The flood was coming. No one had seen it start, or known what whistling storm made on the dam the final assault. Long before it was manifest to the tribe an intermittent trickle of salt water coursed through the breach, deepening and widening it with every tide, and ran down the bed of the western river to merge at last with the Salt Lake. The animals saw the new river, dark with the muddy spoils of its conquest, and snorted in amazement at its unpleasant taste. The blacks saw it and perhaps marveled for a space. The migratory birds, coursing over it in their thousands, paid it no heed, just as they paid none later to the sea that followed it. But no word of it had reached the tribe. Day and night it grew, as the torrent swelled in strength and depth and speed, fed by all the oceans of the globe.

It was only when the Salt Lake had spread to thrice its former width, and had approached within two days' march of the village, that Milis discovered it, and by that time the breach at Gibraltar was almost as wide as it is today, and the surging waters were licking the bases of the two giant rocks. Trees, soil, stones and clay had long ago been thrown aside like dust, and, day by day, the waters scoured deeper into the underlying rock, already undermined and weakened by centuries of penetrating streamlets.

Now Milis was clutching the trembling old shoulder, crying, again and again, "Your flood, Andor, your flood!"

Andor was on his feet. With strength that she did not know he had, his fingers gripped her soft shoulder for support, his other thin hand shading his eyes against the southern sun. "Where? Where? I can't see. Where?" he demanded.

Stor, too, was on his feet, staring. "Nonsense," he growled. "There isn't any flood."

Now Andor's eyes cleared. Yes, there it was. There where he had always known it would be. Andor's flood—his own flood—his friend, the flood.

It was hard to remember, now, the terror that had swept through him when he first conceived the thought. It had really taken courage, he recalled, to walk down that slope after his first discovery, turning his back on the cold death that lurked behind the pass. Almost with a smile he thought of the days and years of trepidation, revealed to none but Bardis, through which he had lived. All that was gone. Now that the flood was really coming, he felt for it a curious bitter comradeship. That it would reach him and encompass him in its lethal waters he knew, for his wearied frame could never survive the flight to the hills. But in the flood he would find an ironic comprehension. His adversary, while conquering him, would nonetheless prove the full measure of his worth. Here would be no questioning of truth or lie, no carping at details and personalities. Nothing could now conceal the clarity of the facts, since all the veils of doubt and criticism, of rivalry and jealousy, of disbelief and groundless faith, had fallen at Truth's feet. He spread his arms toward the shining streak of water, and the smile that had struggled within him came forth.

"You must go to warn them, Milis," he said. "Go down to the village. Tell boys to run after the hunters—after Mendi and the hunters. Tell Mendi—he will understand what to do. Tell your mother."

"Yes, Andor." Milis was quivering under his grasp, and her eyes were frightened. "Yes, I'll tell them."

"Tell them nothing," rumbled Stor. "Andor, you're a fool, and so is your girl here. That's no flood. That's only one of those dream-lakes that one sees on the desert by the Salt

Lake. I've seen them often, and they never deceived me. Can't you tell a dream-lake from real water? You're a fool. Here, girl, stop! Stop, I say! Don't go down there frightening people. It's only a dream-lake."

He made a clumsy little run as if to catch Milis, but Andor stepped in his way. The girl ran a few steps, and stopped, uncertain. "Run, Milis!" cried Andor. Stor flung him aside with astonishing strength. As Andor stumbled and fell, he thrust his staff between Stor's legs, and brought him also to the ground.

Milis was in terror. Should she run to warn the people? If she did, Stor might hurt Andor, might well kill him in his anger. But the flood—her children! She ran, and Stor rose to his hands and knees to bellow after her "Stop, girl! Stop, fool!"

Andor had regained his feet, but Stor, more shaken than he would admit by the fall, remained in his absurd posture. Andor, looking at him, felt a sudden pity. Stor was beaten at last—was beaten and would die, like all of them. Could he hate him now?

"It isn't a dream-lake, Stor," he said. "Look at it carefully."

Stor looked, and after a while rose painfully to his feet, still staring. "Is that your flood?" he asked at last, in a small voice that trembled.

"That's the flood, Stor. And now we must go down to the village, to help them all make ready to flee. Perhaps we can escape it."

"But you didn't tell us it was coming now," protested Stor.

**177**

"You didn't explain. How can we get ready now, when it's nearly here?"

While Stor babbled on, Andor was walking—nay, almost striding—down the short slope to the village, and Stor had eventually to save his breath to keep up with him. Once in the double circle of houses they were surrounded by a crowd of chattering women, and children of all ages.

Quickly Milis and Andis saw that the questioning was too much for Andor's strength. While Milis found him a seat, Andis spoke to the circle of women. As she spoke, the hunters began arriving from the fields.

"It's Andor's flood," she shouted. "The flood that he has always said would come. Perhaps you don't remember, but that doesn't matter now it's here. Pack up what you can, each of you—hides, tools, weapons, and food. But hurry, and don't take too big a load. It will be a long, hard march."

Mendi came and stood before Andor, his chest heaving from his run. "So it's come, Father," he said. "Have we time to make ready?"

"I don't know, Mendi. I don't know how fast it can come. Hurry. Perhaps there will be time."

"Good, we're almost ready. Come along."

"I'm not going," said Andor.

Mendi stared at his father. He saw him as he had always known him, and yet he seemed to realize for the first time how old he was. With a shock of surprise he looked at the bent, frail shoulders, the shrunken ribs, the deep-wrinkled cheeks above the snowy beard.

"Not going?" he repeated dully.

**178**

"No," said Andor. "My heart would fail before the marches you must take, and my old legs would serve but to delay you, when delay is not safe.

"Besides, my work is done. I have not saved the tribe, but I have pointed out to a few of you—to my own children, at least—how you may be able to save yourselves. You know the road to the cave, and you know how to find the game there. You will be able to help such as follow you to find a foothold in the new life. But for me, life was finished when first the flood appeared. I shall stay here and see the end."

"But the whole tribe is fleeing, Father. No one will stay behind to be caught by the water. Of course you will come with us."

There was a finality in the old man's look that stole the strength from his son's words. Helplessly and automatically he turned to gather up his people. Then he returned to where the old man stood, gazing over the blue distances of the south. The declining sun warmed the colors of the land with rose and purple, and the approaching coolness of the evening smoothed out care.

"We are going, Father," said the younger man. His face above the jungled beard was grave and lined, but still composed.

"Then farewell, Mendi. Be swift to avoid the waters. I will not keep you. Are the others going?"

"Only our family, Father," Mendi looked puzzled. "The others say they must go, but they will not start at sunset, or they cannot find their weapons, or they have not enough food. Tomorrow I think they will all go. I have told them tomorrow will be too late, but they pay no heed."

"They never have, my boy, and I did not expect them to begin now. I think you will escape if you start now—but I do not know how those will fare who start tomorrow. So good-by, my son."

One by one the old man's clan came to him for a hand-clasp or an embrace, and when the last was gone Mendi went, too.

As Mendi had said, only a handful of the tribe left for the mountains that evening, in spite of Andor's tireless urging, and of that handful some of the stragglers made only a few miles before camping for the night. In the dark it seemed foolish to be fleeing this invisible danger, for the warm heavens were as friendly and familiar as ever, and the soft night noises of the plains could inspire no terror of the unknown. Only Mendi and his little band marched through the night, pushing north and west on the path Andor had planned, and they only rested a few hours at daybreak before pushing on again. With the dawn they could see the waters near at hand, but they also could feel themselves gaining. At last, their strength almost gone, the men carrying the weeping, exhausted children, they reached the high ground that meant safety.

In the village it was otherwise. Just as the dove-gray eastern clouds washed the plain with daylight, the water appeared. For a space the river grew stagnant, and splashed uncertainly in the fringing reeds, feeling its doom. Then the rush of the sea overwhelmed it, and eddied about the foundations of the village wall. Through the gates, and through the gaps that appeared as pieces of the wall collapsed, the brown flood sucked and gurgled around the mud houses. With shrieks and imprecations, with terror in eyes and hands, the people fled.

At first they tried to follow up the river bank, in the direction Mendi and his people had taken, but the advancing tide was too swift for them and they were forced to the higher ground. By noon the sea stretched far ahead of them, up the valley, and they retreated eastward toward the gently swelling ridge that lay between the river and the Red Mountains.

Then Konor, who was running ahead, came to the highest point of the ridge, and saw the waters before him. A swift glance around showed him that they were trapped—that the ridge had become an island. His cries gathered the fleeing people, and they clustered about him. Far behind, forgotten by the others in their panic, came Stor and Andor, struggling against the slope and against the lassitude of their aged limbs. As they walked they helped each other forward, and neither spoke.

On the hilltop, sharply cut against the sky, washed by the sunlight of a smiling afternoon, stood the people of the tribe. Near them roved restless bands of gazelles and horses, and through the thigh-deep grasses slunk wolves and foxes. Beyond them a shaggy mammoth trumpeted his fear, and backed step by step from the encroaching waves. The grass was alive with little animals of all sorts, and birds crowded each other on the twigs of the scattered trees. Over it all

**181**

*The old man stood, gazing over the blue distances of the south.*

**182**

183

the gentle breeze, newly salt to the nostrils, rustled the ripe grass. Blue and serene, its surface ruffled by the wind, its ripples juggling scraps of sunlight, the ocean lay around them. Far across it, clear in the afternoon light, stood the ranked mountain ridges, their ice fields catching a glitter from the declining sun. Except for the panic-stricken animals, and the huddled speechless people, the beautiful evening came on in perfect peace—the peace of the end.

For a space the waters paused, as if toying cruelly with their victims. Had Andor's travels taken him farther afield he would have known the reason. Beyond the Fire Mountains of Sicily, beyond the vanished Salt Lake of the southern deserts, there had lain another great valley. Its branches had spread among the ragged hills of Greece, and behind the green Appenines of Italy. In it had stood the tall ranges of Crete and Cyprus, and in its center had lain a huge sea-like lake, fed by the waters of the Danube, the Volga, and the Nile.

Now the sea had broken into this second valley, and gradually the Mediterranean as the Phoenicians knew it, was taking shape. The advancing waves engulfed the rivers as the sea grew, until the Danube and the Volga were pushed back to the Black Sea, and the Nile was stopped midway in its burning valley.

A third valley, much smaller than the others, escaped the

inundation. As the sea crept up to the gray shores of Palestine, the wandering tribes of hunters who dwelt there took refuge in the remaining valley behind the sheltering mountains, where the waters of the Jordan tumbled over boulders and gravel into the salty sea that even then was called Dead. Among those people bards sang of the flood, and so began a story that has lived longer on the tongues of men than any other.

In their brief respite on the new-made island, the tribe lived a curious dreamlike existence. Food, of course, was easy to obtain, for the grassy uplands teemed with frightened game. Wolves prowled ceaselessly around the camp, and constant watch had to be kept for them. Given enough time, it is possible that a new life might have been designed that would have lifted the terror from their minds, and allowed at least some of them to survive on the island. But time was not given. When the next slim moon was born the waters again advanced, having filled to the brim the second valley behind the Fire Mountains. More slowly this time, but with terrifying sureness, the waves crept through the grass, shrinking the island of refuge hour by hour.

As night fell, Andor walked alone by the lisping water. He had ceased to hear the wails of the despairing people, and he paid no heed to the rustlings and scamperings of frightened animals. He fixed his eyes on the moon, sinking toward the jagged edge of the unattainable mountains of the west.

A long path of glittering jewels stretched from his feet to those distant peaks, and to that silver door that was opening for him into the land of the dead. Over the path walked Kelan, his eyes dancing with youthful laughter, limping a little on his wounded leg. With him came Bardis, and the moonlight that glanced from her dark hair was like the shimmer of the wavelets under her feet. In her eyes there was no weariness, no pain, and no longing, but only quiet and understanding love.

Andor straightened his frail shoulders, and from them the years and the weariness fell off as fall an athlete's garments. With welcoming arms he met them, and strode confidently forth between them toward the radiant moon-door in the sky. And when the people sought him, with cries of terror and reproach and helplessness, they found him not.

# AUTHOR'S NOTE

"And The Waters Prevailed" is a story, told only for its interest as a story.

It is not a treatise on anthropology. Scholars can correct me on the tribal organization and customs of *Homo sapiens sapiens* at the ending of the Ice Age, if they know, and I will be happy to learn from them. But I believe that people have not changed much in these latest few thousand years of man's million year history, and that they *might* have lived and acted as the people in my story did. And I don't think the scholars will contradict that.

Nor is it a geological monograph. That the Mediterranean was formed by a breach at Gibraltar, letting the rising Atlantic flood a lowland basin, seems very probable; the date of this dramatic event, however, is utterly uncertain. Most probably it happened before man stood on his hind legs and ceased being an ape. But it *could* have happened at the end of the Ice Age. That it gave rise to the Biblical story of the Flood, as I suggest, seems highly unlikely, since Sir Leonard Woolley's distinguished work—but the suggestion is meant to call attention to the similarity between today's closed basins, like the Caspian, the Dead Sea and Egypt's Q'atara, and yesterday's, like the Mediterranean and the Red Sea.

That Cro-Magnon or Chancellade men moved from their caves in the Pyrenees to the doomed valley, is pure story-

*187*

telling. Many other explanations of their disappearance are probably more likely—including the possibility that they never disappeared at all but are living today (or their descendants are) in the Provence and Catalonia.

If I have pictured that ancient time convincingly, if I have made Andor and Stor and Bardis live in the reader's mind, if by my tale I have held your interest, and perhaps opened a crack of the door to further learning, my tale has done what it set out to do.

D. MOREAU BARRINGER
*Philadelphia, 1956*